She could hear his heart beating and wondered if he could hear the wild pounding of her own heart—but it was not from fear. Without knowing why, she trusted him implicitly. Then his lips were touching the corner of her mouth, still light as butterflies. . . . She felt the same sensation she'd experienced in the gallery. As naturally as though she'd done it a thousand times, Gillian lifted her arms around his neck.

Slowly, Leo warned himself as she willingly accepted his embrace. He kissed her, gently at first, just touching her lips with the tip of his tongue. When she responded, he deepened the kiss, and was surprised by the sudden surge of desire he felt. Abruptly he released her and stepped back. . . .

By Jeanne Carmichael
Published by Fawcett Books:

LORD OF THE MANOR
LADY SCOUNDREL
A BREATH OF SCANDAL
FOREVER YOURS
MISS SPENCER'S DILEMMA
AN INCONVENIENT MARRIAGE

AN INCONVENIENT MARRIAGE

Jeanne Carmichael

FAWCETT CREST • NEW YORK

A Fawcett Crest Book
Published by Ballantine Books
Copyright © 1997 by Carol Quinto

http://www.randomhouse.com

Library of Congress Catalog Card Number: 96-97060

ISBN 0-449-22467-8

Manufactured in the United States of America

First Edition: January 1997

10 9 8 7 6 5 4 3 2 1

Chapter 1

At half past two on Monday afternoon, Gillian Prescott strode out of Mrs. Dunstone's home with such vigor, the silk skirt of her fashionable walking dress whipped against her slender legs. The color was high in the lady's cheekbones, and she had to bite her lower lip to keep from voicing her displeasure.

Several paces behind her, Mrs. Ledbetter struggled to keep up. "Gillian! Gillian, my dear, do slow down. 'Tis most unseemly to be seen hurrying so. Why, if anyone were to see you, they would think—"

"I do not care what anyone thinks," Gillian snapped, whirling to face the elderly woman engaged as her companion. "I did not wish to come to London, and as soon as I see Papa, I intend to ask him to send me home to Richmond on the first ship that sails."

"Oh, my dear, pray do not say so. If you will only reflect a moment, I am sure you will see that Mrs. Connell meant nothing by her remarks. I am convinced she did not know you had come up behind her—"

Gillian impatiently waved away her companion's remarks. "Mrs. Connell was not the only one. Every one of those ladies despised me, but I assure you, I do not regard that in the least. Jealous cats, all of them, and the gentlemen little better. I shall go home to Willowglen, where people are treated with courtesy, and rank does not give any person the right to be . . . to be rude," she

1

finished, her voice rising. But for all her brave words, she was very near to tears, and blindly spun around to seek the privacy of her carriage.

She collided with a gentleman in the buff and silver uniform of one of the cavalry regiments. She had a brief impression of a solid chest, muscular strength, and an enticing scent that put her much in mind of the lawn at Willowglen after a spring rain. Capable hands caught her up before she could slip, and set her firmly on the path. Gillian looked up, her gaze traveling above the thread-bare collar, above the firm, square-cut chin, to meet a pair of amused deep-set gray eyes beneath dark, heavy brows.

Suspecting that he was laughing at her, Gillian stepped back and muttered, "Are you so anxious to visit Mrs. Dunstone that you must run me down?"

"I rather thought it was the other way around," he replied, taken aback by her obvious anger.

"Well, if you will block the walk—!"

"American?" he asked, catching the Southern cadence that drew out her words and that, despite her anger, added a softness to her voice. "I do not believe I've had the pleasure, Miss . . . ?"

The elderly woman engaged as a companion stepped forward, but Gillian glared her into silence, answering the gentleman herself. "We have not been properly introduced, sir, and I believe, according to your barbaric English customs, it is therefore most improper of you to accost me. Pray excuse me."

"Accost you? Why, of all the—" But he was left talking to air as the small American swept past him in a swirl of silken skirts. Her companion, head down, followed, and both were assisted into an elaborate town coach by a footman clad in a heavily embellished livery of green, gold, and silver.

Captain Leopold Reed, currently home on furlough

2

from the 52nd Regiment, shrugged off the incident. Americans had no manners and, judging from the remarks he'd overheard, this particular one had managed to offend the ladies gathered at Mrs. Dunstone's home, not that it mattered greatly. He could have told her, had she been civil enough to listen, that her hostess and her acquaintances were not among the ton, and their opinion of little importance to those who counted in London. But it was, after all, no concern of his, and he had pressing matters enough to worry him.

He strode to the door, but before his hand could lift the knocker, it was opened by a portly butler.

"My Lord Wrexham! May I say, my lord, that 'tis indeed a pleasure to welcome you home. Mr. Dunstone told me to be on the watch for you, and he is waiting in the library. If you will come with me, my lord?"

As he followed the man down the long hall, Leo limped slightly, the result of an old wound that seemed to afflict him anew whenever he overexerted himself or felt unduly disturbed. He knew the cause today was the latter, for he was not looking forward to this interview with Dunstone. As he passed the winding staircase that led to the upper stories, the sound of feminine voices floated down. He paid no attention. There was only one lady in London that he desired to see, and it was extremely unlikely he would meet her in this house. Miss Diana Beauclerk moved only in the first circles. Just as well, Leo thought wryly, knowing that he must put all thought of her from his mind.

The butler paused before a paneled door, tapped lightly, then opened it for his lordship. He would have liked to have entered the room and announced Lord Wrexham's presence in deep, resounding tones—for it was seldom gentlemen of rank visited—but Mr. Dunstone had given him orders to quietly admit his lordship and withdraw. Reluctantly, Forest pulled the door shut.

3

William Dunstone, a thin gentleman of an indeterminate age who might be anywhere between forty and sixty, glanced up at the intrusion. When he saw who had entered, he hurriedly rose to his feet, then circled around the desk to extend his hand in a warm welcome. "Lord Wrexham, come in, come in, sir. I realize 'tis a sad occasion which brings you home, my lord, and pray you accept my deepest condolences."

"Thank you," Leo replied, still uncomfortable with the title, which seemed to sit heavily on his shoulders. He had not expected to step into his father's shoes so soon, and it would be some time before he would answer readily to anything but Captain Reed. He accepted the chair offered, then fastened his level gaze on his host. "It was kind of you to agree to see me so promptly."

Dunstone sighed deeply as he seated himself behind his desk. "I only wish circumstances were different. To lose both your father and your brother in one stroke—it does not bear thinking of. I was not privileged to know your brother, but I had extensive dealings with your father. May I say, my lord, that he was extremely proud of you, and would have wished to welcome you home in style. It was always so. I can recollect his bragging of your prowess even when you were still in the cradle."

Leo smiled dutifully, but in truth, he knew little about his father. The fourth Earl of Wrexham, an intimate of the Prince Regent's, had seldom spent time at home, and when he did do so, it was with John, his elder son and heir. He may have spoken warmly of Leo, but he had swept in and out of his life with the force of a tidal wave, leaving behind only fleeting impressions.

"But you are not here to listen to an old man's memories," Dunstone said, recalling that his guest had requested an interview to discuss rather urgent business affairs. "I have heard the rumors. How badly are you left?"

4

"It could not be much worse," Leo admitted. "If only I had known—!"

"Now, don't be blaming yourself, my lord. Your father didn't want you or your brother to know he was in dun territory. He thought to make a recovery, and I believe he might have done so were it not for this unfortunate accident. He had some astonishing runs of luck. 'Tis not the way I would have—but there, talking pays no tolls. Only tell me how I may be of help."

Leo withdrew a slip of paper from his pocket and laid it on the desk. "I found this among my father's papers. He was, at least, meticulous in keeping track of his debts. I realize it is already past due, but if you would allow me a little more time, I assure you that I—"

"Good Lord, that note was paid several weeks ago. I wonder your father did not record it—"

"No, sir. It was not paid, and although it is exceedingly kind and most generous of you to pretend otherwise, I cannot allow it."

William Dunstone flushed. He was a kindhearted man, and had been sincerely fond of the fourth Earl of Wrexham. But he was also a shrewd banker. It was not the first time he had advanced the old lord funds. Dunstone had always been paid eventually, but even if he'd had to weather a loss, it would have been worth it for the standing it gave him among his colleagues in the city. To be known as Wrexham's friend was no slight thing.

"Throw it in the fire," he suggested, looking up to meet the new earl's level gaze. "I can stand the nonsense easily, and 'tis one last thing I can do for your father."

"I would prefer you allow me a fortnight's grace," Leo replied, a shade stiffly. "I've discussed matters with Halthorpe, my man of business, and I hope that by practicing some economies and selling off everything possible, I shall eventually emerge free of debt. The racing stable and the town house will be put on the block next

5

week, and if all goes well, I shall redeem my father's vowel then."

"I will not presume to advise you, my lord, but, good heavens, I must say I cannot think such a move advisable! Surely your man told you that if you sell the stables, your creditors will be on you like a swarm of locusts. It will act as a signal that you are badly dipped and—"

"The truth will out?" Leo interrupted. "Unfortunately, I see little choice and little point in concealing that it's high tide with me. The news will spread when I put Farthingale on the market."

Dunstone's jaw dropped. He had never been privileged to visit Wrexham's seat, but he knew it had been in the Reed family for countless generations, and he'd heard numerous tales of the lavish entertainments given at Farthingale. Royalty frequently visited the estate, and it was believed that Bonny Prince Charles had once taken refuge in the ancient ruins. Selling it was unthinkable. Why, it was like . . . like old King George suddenly taking it into his head to sell off Windsor, or the Regent putting Carleton House on the market.

Shaken, Dunstone rose and crossed to the sideboard, where he kept various decanters. He poured out a generous measure of brandy for both himself and Wrexham. "I do not know what to say, my lord. I knew your father was under the hatches, but that it must come to selling Farthingale—surely there must be another way to recover."

Leo laughed dryly. "If you can think of one, I wish you would tell me so. I need not scruple to tell you, sir, that my mother is all to pieces over the news. But I have her and Clarissa to provide for . . ." Remembering the distraught face of his younger sister, Leo drained half his glass. He'd learned fighting on the Peninsula that life was seldom fair, but she was too young to be so disillusioned, too young to have her hopes for a good marriage so brutally dashed.

William Dunstone suddenly recalled a conversation he'd had some days ago, and it occurred to him that there might be a way for his lordship to save his home . . . if Wrexham was willing. He studied the gentleman before him. Although they'd met on several occasions, they'd had no business dealings. Still, he was of the opinion that the new earl was a levelheaded, sensible young man. If he could be brought to set aside his pride, it just might be possible . . .

Making up his mind, Dunstone leaned across the desk. "My lord, will you refrain from taking any action for a few days? I don't wish to raise your hopes unreasonably, but there is a possibility I could set you in the way of saving Farthingale."

Leo's brows rose. "If you are thinking of picking up the mortgages, it is extremely kind of you, but I cannot think of taking on another debt."

"No, no—nothing like that. Just grant me a day or two. Are you staying in Grosvenor Square?"

"The Belle Sauvage," Leo answered, naming an inn conveniently situated on Ludgate Hill. "I did not want to open the town house for the short time I shall be in London."

"Then I'll send a note around to the inn if something comes of this." Feeling more cheerful by the moment, Dunstone refilled their glasses. "In the meantime, I beg you not to regard your father's note. If you will not allow me to destroy it entirely, at least let it be the last of the debts you pay."

"You are very good, sir."

Dunstone denied it, knowing it was little enough he was offering. He wished he could do more, but young Wrexham had his pride. He wouldn't accept a loan, or help with the mortgages—he might not agree to the

7

scheme Dunstone had in mind, even if Prescott was willing, which was not at all certain.

Lord Wrexham dined Wednesday evening at the Belle Sauvage Inn in a private sitting room. He had declined an invitation to join a few of his friends at White's. So much had changed since his return, and although he tried to accept his reduced circumstances with good grace, he did not feel he could endure the sympathetic looks and murmurs of condolences from his friends—not just yet.

The realization that he would have to sell Farthingale had, however improperly, distressed him far more than the sad news of his father's passing and that of his brother's. It was not that he was unfeeling, but he had become somewhat hardened to death during the campaign on the Peninsula, and the truth was, his father and John had been little more than strangers. Farthingale, however, was his home. He had grown to manhood within its weathered stone walls, and he had felt it would always be there, waiting to welcome him back. The thought of Farthingale in someone else's possession was almost unbearable.

Still, there seemed no other way. Leo sighed as he allowed the waiter to refill his coffee cup. He lit a cigar and was contemplating a stroll to try to escape the gloom pervading his spirits when the innkeeper tapped on the door, then looked in. "Your pardon, my lord, but there's a . . . a person wishful of a word with you."

It was obvious from the innkeeper's disapproving manner that the caller was not a respectable one. No doubt another creditor to dun him. Leo waved a hand and issued instructions to send the fellow on his way. But when the innkeeper remained by the table, he glanced up, brows raised. "Well? What are you waiting for?"

"The thing is, my lord, 'tis a young lady what wishes a word with you. I would've sent her off with a flea in her ear, but though she talks funny, she's well dressed, and she said as 'ow she met your lordship Monday past at Mr. Dunstone's home. Miss Prescott, she said her name was."

Leo hesitated. The name meant nothing to him, but he did remember calling on Dunstone Monday, and he also recalled the little American who had careened into him as she was leaving the house. He thought it unlikely that she would visit him at his hotel, but he was curious enough to tell the innkeeper to send the lady in.

He'd risen to his feet when the door opened and a petite lady clad in a hooded cloak entered the room. She came in hesitantly, as though fearing someone might jump out and attack her. Delusional, Leo thought, observing her small upturned nose liberally sprinkled with freckles. Her mouth was a fraction too wide, and her reddish hair—which had been severely restrained on Monday—now tumbled about her face in a riot of curls. Her only redeeming feature was a pair of wide-set blue eyes. She regarded him gravely, and Leo stepped forward. "Miss Prescott?"

"You must think it most strange of me to call on you in this manner," she said, but there was no hint of apology in her words. Indeed, her stance and her tone were almost a challenge.

Leo thought it fifty-fifty whether she stayed or bolted. He smiled down at her. "I confess, I am rather curious. Will you be seated and tell me how I may be of service to you?"

Seeming to make up her mind, she advanced into the room and settled herself at the table. When he had resumed his own place, she folded her hands primly, lifted her chin, and informed him, "I do not wish you to be of service. That, my lord, is what I came to tell you."

Were all Americans mad? Leo wondered. He nobly resisted an impulse to laugh, but he couldn't help the amusement that lingered in his voice as he replied, "I shall bear your wishes in mind should I ever be in a position to render you assistance."

The blue eyes studied him gravely. After a moment, she asked doubtfully, "You *are* Lord Wrexham?"

"I am," he agreed.

She shook her head slightly as though to clear the confusion that suddenly shadowed her eyes. "You returned home recently and discovered your estates were heavily encumbered?"

"You seem to know a great deal about me," he replied, no longer quite so amused.

"My father said that he . . . he spoke to you. He offered you the means of saving your home—"

"I hate to disillusion you, Miss Prescott, but I am not acquainted with your father."

Color flooded her cheeks. "Then he has not spoken to you yet. My lord, I must apologize. I would not have ventured to come here, but I thought—" She broke off, rising abruptly to her feet. "The situation seemed most urgent, but perhaps Papa changed his mind. Forgive me for disturbing you, my lord."

She reminded him of a bird, ready to fly if one approached too quickly. Leo rose to his feet, and sought to ease her embarrassment. "You did not disturb me in the least, Miss Prescott. I was merely sitting here wallowing in self-pity, which I can tell you is not at all conducive to improving one's spirits. Your unexpected visit is, in truth, a welcome reprieve from my own miserable thoughts, and I would consider it an honor if you would bear me company yet awhile."

Her chin lifted, and the blue eyes flashed. All prickly, he thought. The little bird had talons.

"You need not patronize me, Lord Wrexham. I know full well it was wrong of me to call. None of your English ladies would do such a thing."

"I cannot gainsay you, Miss Prescott. Given my present circumstances, it is highly likely the English ladies of my acquaintance will avoid me like the plague, but that does not lessen my pleasure in receiving you. I meant what I said."

"Do you mean the ladies you know will avoid you merely because your father foolishly lost his fortune?"

Leo regretted the impulse that had led him to try to comfort this strange minx. He might curse his father's extravagance, but he very much disliked hearing anyone else do so. Even more, he was irrationally angry that anyone would criticize, however obliquely, Miss Diana Beauclerk. He curbed his annoyance and replied with tolerable composure, "I did not mean to imply that anyone would cut me directly, but certainly you must understand that I can no longer be considered a desirable suitor."

"Oh, humbug."

"I beg your pardon?" Leo said, putting up his brows.

"I suppose I should not have said that, either, but in Virginia we have no truck with titles and such. A gentleman is judged by what he accomplishes—not what his father did or left to him—which to my mind seems a much more sensible way of looking at things. If you don't mind my saying so, my lord, you English have some rather odd customs."

Leo gestured toward the chair. His leg was paining him, and he told her, "If we are going to continue this conversation, Miss Prescott, will you not be seated? One of our odd customs is that a gentleman may not sit while a lady stands."

She hesitated, but then sat rather primly on the edge of the chair. "Thank you, my lord. I did not mean to sound critical. Mrs. Ledbetter tells me it puts one's back up when I speak of how we do things at home, but it tries my patience sorely when I hear people talking as if they'd no more sense than a pig in a poke."

Amused, he wondered if she were referring to him. He looked down at her red curls and remarked, "Somehow, I suspect patience is not one of your long suits."

Her mouth stretched into a wide grin that turned her countenance into a pleasing one. She had the look of a pixie, Leo thought, or a mischievous imp.

"Papa says my temper is one of my worst faults, and I know 'tis so. Sometimes the words just tumble out. I *know* I should think before I speak, but it is very difficult. Do you understand what I mean, my lord?"

Leo, a model of stoic British composure, did not. From the cradle up, he'd been taught that one maintained a facade of civilized, dignified behavior in public. It was second nature to him. Even on the Peninsula, in the heat of battle, he'd never vented the anger he'd felt when a subordinate disobeyed orders, or recklessly risked the lives of his men. He might rake the man down in private, but even then it was with a controlled anger.

"No, I can see you do not," she remarked, her head tilted to one side.

"My lamentable upbringing," he murmured. "May I offer you a glass of ratafia or sherry?"

Her tiny nose wrinkled in distaste. "A mint julep I would accept, and very much enjoy, but that stuff the ladies drink here—I apologize, my lord. I am doing it again, am I not? Criticizing what's offered, when you only meant to be kind."

"Do not apologize, Miss Prescott. The truth is, I cannot abide ratafia myself, but if this mint julep you mentioned is an American drink, I fear the innkeeper will not be able to prepare it."

"He won't, take my word for it, but it scarce matters, for I cannot stay. I have to return home before Papa. He would have my head on a platter if he knew I had come here."

Reminded of the purpose of her visit, Leo asked,

"Why did you come? I gather your father had some proposition to lay before me, although how he came to hear of me, or why he should trouble himself over my affairs, has me in a puzzle."

"It was Mr. Dunstone," Gillian confided. "He is a friend of Papa's, and he had some notion that—" She broke off, blushing a fiery red. Avoiding his gaze, she continued, "Mr. Dunstone thought that if you married an heiress, you need not sell your home."

"I'm beginning to see," Leo replied curtly. "I apprehend your father is a person of substantial wealth, and you, I gather, have come to tell me that you do not wish to be the . . . sacrificial lamb?" When she confirmed his guess with a hesitant nod, he rose stiffly to his feet. "You may rest easy, Miss Prescott. Should your father approach me, I shall certainly tell him that I have no desire to enter into a marriage of convenience."

He spoke quietly, but his eyes held a coldness that chilled Gillian to the bone. She bit her lip, knowing that she had somehow offended him.

"Allow me to escort you to your carriage," he added with icy politeness.

Even while standing, Gillian had to tilt her head back to gaze up into his eyes. Her own were filled with remorse as she drawled softly, "Pray forgive me, my lord."

Some of the stiffness left Leo. However galling it was to think of his personal affairs being discussed with a . . . a merchant, it was not this child's fault. He swallowed his pride and forced a smile to his lips. "You have nothing to apologize for, Miss Prescott. I can only imagine your dismay when you learned of your father's plan to wed you to a penniless lord. May I say that I admire your courage in coming here?"

"More like panic," she confided in her relief that he no longer seemed so angry. "But it was not you I objected to . . . I mean, I think any lady who married you would

13

be most fortunate. 'Tis just that I have no wish to wed an Englishman. 'Tis plain I don't belong here. I miss Willowglen something dreadful."

There was no mistaking the poignancy of her voice or the unhappiness in her wide blue eyes. She was homesick. He'd dealt with dozens of young men in his command who had experienced the same desperate yearnings for home. He had even felt it himself on a few occasions. Knowing that it would help her to talk, he suggested gently, "Tell me about this place you call Willowglen."

She was still talking about the stone house that sat on the banks of the St. James River, and the beautiful willow trees that surrounded it, when they reached the door leading out to Ludgate Hill. He half listened, glancing with concern at the nearly deserted street. When she paused for breath, he inquired politely, "Where is your carriage?"

"I hired a hackney," Gillian explained, looking distractedly around. "But he would not wait. I thought I could find another . . ."

"Stay here," Leo ordered, and gestured to one of the postilions lingering near the door. He instructed the lad to have his own carriage brought around at once, then turned to his visitor. "Will you allow me the honor of driving you home, Miss Prescott?"

She blushed, the fiery red coloring her face seeming to deepen the flaming red of her curls. "I cannot impose on you, but if you could help me find a carriage, I would be much obliged."

"I doubt very much if there is one to be had at this hour." The lamps on the street were lit, and most of the town's inhabitants were at home. In another hour the street would be thick with carriages, but for now it was peacefully quiet. Smiling down at the slender girl beside him, Leo teased, "Surely you can have no objection to driving with me? Not when we were nearly betrothed."

Gillian choked back an urge to giggle wildly. How absurd he was! But her amusement was short-lived as she thought of her father and how furious he would be were he to return home and find her gone, without even her maid to lend her countenance. She had no time to waste. "If you are certain it will not be too much trouble," she murmured.

"None at all," Leo assured her as his carriage was brought up. He helped her in, then took the reins himself. He had neither groom nor tiger with him, but after being alone with Miss Prescott in the Belle Sauvage for nearly an hour, it was a little late to be thinking of the proprieties.

Chapter 2

Oliver Prescott paced the floor of the spacious drawing room on the lower floor of the house he'd leased in Cavendish Square. Although he admired the pretty design of the square and the fenced-in fountain opposite the house, and had been assured by Mrs. Ledbetter and various acquaintances that the location was a fashionable one, he still thought the place rather plain. But, at the moment, he was too preoccupied over the disappearance of his daughter to pay heed to his surroundings.

Mrs. Ledbetter, seated on the cream and rose serpentine sofa, sipped her tea and watched him warily. Fearing that her employer would blame her for Gillian's disappearance, she said for the fourth time, "I vow I cannot understand it. Gillian told me she intended to rest before dinner and did not wish to be disturbed before your return. I was shocked, utterly shocked, to find her gone, and why she should choose to step out alone when I have told her dozens of times that no lady goes abroad in London without her maid, I cannot conceive."

Oliver, a large, barrel-chested man with a florid countenance and graying hair, glowered at her. "What I cannot conceive is how, in a house of this paltry size, she could leave without being seen! No less than twenty staff I hired, and not one of them can tell me when Gillian left or where she went. And you, madam—it's your duty to accompany my girl."

"And I would have done so had Gillian seen fit to inform me that she wished to go out," the lady replied, plying her fan. "But, as I told you, she never said a word."

"And why is that, I wonder? 'Pears to me that if Gillian thought you a fitting companion, she would've confided in you."

Mrs. Ledbetter wheezed as though her corset were laced too tight. "Really, Mr. Prescott, you are behaving most unjustly. You know as well as I that your daughter is not happy to be in England, and if she will not make an effort to be received here, there is little I can do."

He glared at the small lady. With her stiffly erect back and massive bosom habitually draped in gray, she reminded him strongly of a pouter pigeon. She dropped the names of dukes and earls left and right, but he suspicioned that she had only a nodding acquaintance with the peerage, and he'd been right taken-in by her. He didn't object to paying out good money for what he wanted, but he did resent being choused.

"Perhaps we should send someone to search for her," Mrs. Ledbetter suggested, misliking the look on his face. "Gillian simply may have stepped out for a breath of air and lost her way, or—"

"And you think she has not the sense to ask the direction?" he interrupted furiously. "Why, Gillian has run a house twice this size since she was knee-high to a mosquito and had to use a cushion on her chair just to see over the table. My daughter has more sense in her little finger than you have in your entire body, madam, and if—" He halted mid-tirade as he heard the unmistakable sound of carriage wheels clattering against the cobblestones in front of the house. Muttering a prayer that Gillian had returned safely, he rushed to the windows in time to see his daughter handed down from a landau by a man clad in military raiment.

17

"Oh, thank heavens," Mrs. Ledbetter murmured as she peered over his shoulder.

"For what?" Oliver boomed as relief quickly turned to anger. "A fine thing for my girl to be racketing about Town with one of them regimental fellows. If that's your notion of fitting behavior, madam, I take leave to tell you, it ain't mine."

"No indeed, Mr. Prescott, but if I am not much mistaken, the gentleman is one Gillian met at Mr. Dunstone's. I am quite sure he is perfectly respectable."

"Balderdash!" Oliver roared as he strode toward the door. "I'll have a few things to say to that lad, aye, and to Gillian, as well."

Broom, the elderly butler, stepped back hastily as his employer plunged into the hall and flung open the door. In all his years of service, Broom had never witnessed such undignified conduct. Thoughts of retirement entered his head as he watched Oliver Prescott fly down the steps, bellowing at the top of his lungs.

"Just a minute, young man—I want a word with you. What the devil do you mean by meeting my daughter on the sly?"

"Papa, please," Gillian pleaded, her face flushing a bright red. "It is not what you think—"

"I'll have plenty to say to you in a minute, miss. You get in the house afore I forget you're a young lady and turn you over my knee like you deserve!"

Mortified, she cast an apologetic glance at her escort, then fled up the steps.

"As for you, sir, don't be thinking you can feather your nest at my expense. My daughter might be an heiress, but not a penny does she get if she marries to displease me."

Leo, his brows raised in disbelief, stared at the angry bearlike creature before him. He was more amused than annoyed, and answered politely, "I assure you, sir, that I have no intention of marrying your daughter. I merely—"

An avalanche of fluid curses interrupted him. Leo listened to a blistering tirade that would have done any sergeant-major proud, then stiffened as he heard his character assassinated and was accused of trying to compromise an innocent young girl. When Prescott paused for breath, Leo said quietly, "Are you quite finished, sir?"

"Not by a long shot! Don't let me catch sight of you near this house again, or I'll fill you with buckshot, and that's a promise, lad. I'll not have my daughter ruined by the likes of you!"

Windows were raised at the adjoining houses, and curious heads peeped out as Oliver Prescott vented his wrath. Uncomfortably aware that they were the focus of prying eyes, Leo replied curtly, "You are the one who is likely to ruin your daughter, bandying her name loud enough for all in the square to hear."

"Then, be off with you instead of standing here giving the neighbors something to gawk at," Oliver blustered as he turned back toward the house. He reached the door and added one parting shot over his shoulder, "Remember what I said, my lad—don't show your face here again!"

"You may be sure I won't," Leo muttered as he mounted his carriage. He gave a jaunty salute to Lady Carlisle, who owned the house next to the Prescotts', and had the pleasure of seeing her abruptly shut the window. Then he turned his horses back toward the inn. The fat was in the fire now, he thought, and felt a pang of compassion for Miss Prescott. He hoped she would be able to calm her volatile father before he ruined any chance she had of making a suitable marriage. Poor girl. Small wonder she ached to return to America—with a man like Oliver Prescott for a father, she would never be accepted by the ton.

* * *

19

Inside the house, Gillian waited impatiently for her father. She angrily paced about the drawing room, much as he had done a few minutes earlier. She was furious at having been so humiliated in front of a stranger and felt guilty for leaving Lord Wrexham, who had been the soul of kindness, to face her papa's wrath. But she knew it would have been much worse for him if she'd stayed to argue with her father. When Papa was in such a mood, there was no reasoning with him.

"My dear," Mrs. Ledbetter said, a hint of reproof in her voice, "will you not come sit and compose yourself? Your father was terribly worried when he came home and discovered your absence."

"He did not need to treat me as though I were six. I have never been more embarrassed, and so I shall tell him!"

Mrs. Ledbetter sank into a chair. This was not the first disagreement between her employer and her charge that she'd witnessed. They were both strong-willed, and it was privately her opinion that Gillian had been overly indulged as a child. She had a forthright way of speaking her mind—really quite unbecoming in a young girl. Perhaps it was the red hair . . . or perhaps the influence of those savage Indians she'd heard of in America.

Only the evening before, the dining room had been turned into a battlefield as father and daughter had exchanged bitter words. Mrs. Ledbetter did not entirely approve of Oliver Prescott, but, in her opinion, he had behaved most wisely in trying to arrange a marriage for his wayward daughter. Gillian's objections, she felt, were entirely out of order. It was not as though Mr. Prescott wished her to marry just anyone—he had in mind Lord Wrexham. Why, the girl would be a countess! But Gillian had scorned the notion and begged her father not to force her into a loveless marriage.

Love! These young girls had entirely too much freedom,

to Mrs. Ledbetter's way of thinking. If Gillian had been her daughter, she would not have been permitted to read those dreadful penny novels that filled a girl's head with entirely unsuitable notions of romantic entanglements. But then, what could one expect of an American? The slamming of the front door curtailed Mrs. Ledbetter's thoughts. She braced herself as she heard Prescott's ponderous footsteps approaching.

He shoved open the door and glared at his daughter. "Now, young lady, just what the devil do you mean by disappearing without so much as a word to anyone? It's thankful I am that your mother, the saints preserve her, is not alive to see you slipping off on the sly to meet some soldier."

The color rising in her face, Gillian flung words back at him. "Am I a prisoner then, Papa? Would you keep me confined to my room—"

"Aye, if that's what it takes to keep you from making a bleeding fool of yourself! This is not Richmond, Gillian. You cannot be stepping out alone." He whirled around and exhorted Mrs. Ledbetter, "Tell the girl 'tis the truth I speak. Her reputation will be ruined—"

"Oh, so 'tis my reputation you are worried about?" Gillian interrupted before her companion could speak. With biting sarcasm she continued, "A pity you did not think of my reputation before raking me down in the middle of the square for all our neighbors to hear. I might have entered the house with none the wiser were it not for you yelling, fit to raise the dead—"

"Enough!" Oliver roared. "What would your mother say if she could hear you ranting like a fishwife?"

"Doubtless the same she'd say to you," Gillian replied, but she lowered her voice, knowing her behavior had gone beyond the line. She knew, too, that her gentle mother, had she lived, would have been aghast to hear her speak so. "I beg your pardon, Papa, but you are not being fair. If you would only permit me to explain—"

"Not now," her father replied. His anger spent, he felt suddenly tired and sorely missed his wife. Elizabeth would have known how to deal with their daughter. He sank into the deep cushions of one of the tall wing chairs. "We will talk of this in the morning."

On occasion, Gillian could coax her father into a more pliant mood, but this was not one of those times. She realized that his anger stemmed from concern for her, and he looked so troubled, she felt a pang of remorse. She paused by his chair as she left the room and dropped a light kiss on his head. "I am sorry to have worried you, Papa."

Oliver nodded, but he said nothing further, and after a moment Gillian left the room. When she'd gone, her father sighed. "I don't know what's best to do for her. If I had not promised her mother that I would see her wed to a proper English gentleman, I'd take her back to Virginia tomorrow."

Mrs. Ledbetter blanched. If Gillian returned to America, particularly unwed, her own position would be at an end and she would be unable to use the Prescotts as a reference. Seeking to reassure her employer, she said, "I think, sir, you must not refine overly much on a young girl's romantic notions of marrying for love. Gillian takes her ideas from books, but we, my dear sir, know well the reality of the world. I expect she would be most unhappy living with a penniless young man in a cottage or following the drum were she to take up with a soldier."

"I'd not let her," Oliver answered gruffly. "But the truth is, her mother married me for love. Aye, you may well stare, but Elizabeth came from a genteel family. Her grandfather was a viscount, and she could have done better for herself. Her folks disowned her, for I hadn't a

22

sixpence to my name then. They said she'd married beneath her . . ."

"That may be, Mr. Prescott, but Gillian is in a vastly different position. Why, she is a considerable heiress. It is your duty to protect her, sir."

"Maybe so, but after what she said last night, I had about decided not to approach Lord Wrexham. Now . . . now I just don't know."

"Gillian is a very young and impressionable girl. It is ludicrous to think someone of her age might be wiser than a gentleman as experienced as yourself. Trust me, Mr. Prescott. Your daughter needs a firm hand at this time in her life, and though she might protest now, one day she will thank you. Now, sir, if you will permit me to say so, I expect you are feeling a little peckish. I noticed you did not partake of much at dinner, but Cook has saved back some of the gooseberry pie you so much enjoy. If you will excuse me for a moment, I will have her bring you a slice and a nice bracing cup of tea."

She was gone before he could protest, and she beckoned to one of the footmen waiting in the hall. When she had dispatched him to the kitchens with her instructions, she turned to the butler with a sigh. "I do not scruple to tell you, Mr. Broom, that I have never been employed in such a household. Did you ever see the like—Master going out and ringing a peal over that poor soldier's head for everyone in the square to hear? How he expects me to bring Miss Prescott off creditably is beyond me."

Broom, though he had no high opinion of Mr. Prescott, would not deign to discuss his employer with any of the footmen or maids. He might have unbent with Mrs. Ledbetter, who ranked slightly higher, but he thought her air of consequence pretentious and doubted that she was received in proper London Society. He peered down his long, thin nose at her and took a small bit of pleasure in informing her, "Lord Wrexham is not a mere soldier, madam. He held the rank of captain and, I am given to understand, performed his duties most honorably."

"Wrexham? What has he to—oh, good heavens! Never tell me it was his lordship who brought Miss Prescott home?"

Broom shrugged. "*You* might not recognize him, madam, but Lord Wrexham was a frequent caller at this house in years past. I could not mistake him."

She looked much struck and, after a moment's consideration, muttered, "This changes everything. I must tell Mr. Prescott at once."

She found her employer where she had left him, sitting in the chair near the fireplace. However, he'd had recourse to the brandy decanter and the color had returned to his ruddy cheeks—as well as a touch of belligerence to his eyes. "Tell Cook I don't want any pie," he growled. "All I wish is to be left in peace."

"I think you will change your mind when you hear my news," she replied archly as she advanced into the room.

"Tarnation, woman, are you deaf? I said—"

"Miss Gillian has been compromised!" she interrupted with a dramatic flourish of her hands.

"What the devil do you mean?" Oliver bellowed as he shot to his feet.

Mrs. Ledbetter involuntarily took a step back. "Pray, calm yourself, Mr. Prescott, and allow me to explain. It appears that when Gillian slipped out this evening, she called on Lord Wrexham at his inn. I suppose she may have gone to him with the intention of asking him not to agree to your proposition, but whatever her reason—"

"Bah! I've eyes in my head, and I saw the soldier she was with—"

"Lord Wrexham," she said, raising her voice slightly, "is a soldier. A captain. He was just recently called home from the Peninsula because of his father's death. I doubt he has had sufficient time to order mourning clothes, which is why you mistook him for a common soldier."

Oliver sank back into the chair and reached for his brandy. When he'd recovered a little, he shook his head. "I don't understand it. If that was Wrexham, why didn't he say so? Or Gillian?"

Mrs. Ledbetter remained silent, too tactful to point out that he'd given neither party a chance to say a word.

"Well, I suppose I might as well hang up my fiddle. He ain't going to marry her now, and if word gets about she called on him at his inn, no other gentleman will, either."

"But that is just the point," Mrs. Ledbetter cried. She crossed the room and sat down beside him. "Do you not see, Mr. Prescott? By entertaining Gillian at the inn, Lord Wrexham compromised her. He is honor-bound to wed her whether he wishes to or not!"

Oliver considered the matter, and the more he thought on it, the more pleased he was with the notion. He knew his daughter, knew nothing untoward had passed between her and his lordship. His Gillian might stretch the boundaries of proper behavior, but she would tolerate no dillydallying. But damage had been done her all the same, and it was Wrexham who was at fault. He should have turned her away, refused to see her. By allowing her in and keeping her there, his lordship had indeed compromised his girl, ruined her reputation . . . he would have to do right by her. And Wrexham wouldn't suffer for it—not if what Dunstone had told him about the earl's affairs were true. Oliver was prepared to be generous to him, most generous. As the brandy took effect, he began to think himself very fortunate with the turn his affairs had taken.

"There is just one problem . . ." Mrs. Ledbetter murmured, rudely pulling him from his brandy-induced complacency.

"What's that you say?"

"We have only one problem, sir. Gillian. She may not be receptive to the notion of marrying Lord Wrexham. However, if you are firm with her—"

"Firm?" he muttered, a vision of his blue-eyed daughter coming to mind. He was a shrewd businessman, capable of putting together enormous deals of considerable profit to himself. He'd been described as hard, tough, and knowing. He'd built a fortune of such magnitude that it would take several generations to deplete it, even if he never earned another penny. It was said no man ever got the better of Oliver Prescott, and he knew this to be true. But Gillian was not someone he did business with. She was his only child, the delight of his heart, and when her pretty blue eyes filled with tears, his will of iron turned to mush.

"Firm," Mrs. Ledbetter repeated. "You must not allow your natural partiality for your daughter to dissuade you from doing what is best for her. You must be strong. Insist that she marry Lord Wrexham."

"I'd not want her to be unhappy—"

Mrs. Ledbetter emitted a bark of laughter. "Oh, 'tis indeed prodigious sad for the girl to marry a gentleman like Lord Wrexham! How horrid that she will be a countess with a fine old house, dozens of servants, and a husband as handsome as any girl could wish for!"

Oliver flushed. He had used much the same arguments with his daughter. Only Gillian had countered that she did not want to enter into a marriage with no affection on either side, and that plea had twisted his heart. How could he deny her that which had brought him so much happiness?

"It is what her mother would have wished," Mrs. Ledbetter added softly.

Oliver sighed. Elizabeth had never asked for anything. She'd no fancy for diamonds or pearls or gewgaws of any sort. The house he'd built for her, the servants he'd engaged, had all been appreciated, but were not something she particularly craved. Although she had never once said, Oliver suspected his wife had deeply missed England. They had often spoken of returning for a visit, and her eyes had glowed with pleasure. Only . . . he had waited too long.

He remembered with haunting clarity the way his sweet Elizabeth, with her last breath, had begged him to take Gillian home to England and see her properly wed.

"I'll do it," he announced, coming to a decision. "Tomorrow, I'll call on Lord Wrexham and make the arrangements."

Abovestairs, Gillian sat in the privacy of her bedchamber, pouring out her thoughts and feelings in a crossed and recrossed letter to Anne Patterson, a dear friend from Richmond. Gillian had tried to set down a description of Lord Wrexham and her own surprise at learning he was the soldier she'd met outside Mrs. Dunstone's—the tall, handsome soldier with the gray eyes and reserved manner—but words failed her.

She read what she had written, knew it made no sense, and crumpled the paper. How could she possibly explain that the gentleman who'd made such an impression on her had turned out to be the very man her father had proposed she wed, and whom, she had declared passionately, nothing would induce her to marry.

She had been so surprised when she walked into the Belle Sauvage and saw the soldier instead of the foppish lord she'd expected. Her tongue had tied itself in knots, and though she could not remember precisely what she'd said, she knew it must have been something idiotic. His gray eyes had been amused, just as they had been outside Mrs. Dunstone's.

What was it about him that made her incapable of a coherent thought?

She shook her head as she stared into the flames of the fire burning steadily in the grate. She would never see him again—Papa had made certain of that—so it was a foolish waste of time to sit here thinking of him. She resolutely turned her mind to what lay ahead. For the first time in her life, her father had proven impervious to her entreaties. Gillian had never seen him so determined. At first, when he'd told her he was taking her home to England where she would have a chance to marry a real gentleman, she had not thought him serious.

By the time she realized he meant every word, her beloved Willowglen was announced for sale and a sailing date had been fixed. Gillian had tried tears, pleas, furious arguments, coaxing . . . but nothing had had the least effect on him. He had even threatened to carry her aboard ship if necessary. All because he had promised Mama that he would bring their daughter home to England.

Gillian sighed. It wasn't home to her and never would be. She wasn't like the other young ladies, and she suspected they made fun of her, of the way she talked and dressed and of her boyish figure. After a month in London, Gillian had not one friend.

Despite the fire burning in the grate, she shivered. It was cold this time of year in Richmond, too, but it was a different sort of cold. In London, the dampness seemed to creep into her bones so that she thought she would never get warm. The city was crowded, too, dirty . . . and it got dark so early and stayed dark so long.

A discreet tap on the door intruded on her thoughts, and she heard her maid's husky whisper. Gillian called for the girl to enter.

Lucy slipped in, glancing furtively over her shoulder as though pursued, and cried softly in a voice laden with doom, "Oh, miss!"

Gillian smiled. She'd been wrong. She did have one friend in London in the tall, gangly maid who'd attached herself to Gillian and served her devotedly. It was Lucy who had helped her slip out to meet Lord Wrexham, and Lucy who kept her apprised of what went on in the house.

"Is Papa still in a rage? You needn't worry, Lucy—I will not allow him to turn you off."

"Oh, 'tis worse than that, miss—your papa means to force Lord Wrexham to marry you!"

Gillian stared at her maid. The servants had a habit of listening at doors and knew much more that went on in a household than their masters suspected, but this was absurd. Aloud, she said, "I think you must have misunderstood, Lucy. Judging from what I've seen of his lordship, no one could force him to do anything."

The maid shook her head stubbornly and explained in a rush, "They're saying he compromised you, miss. George heard 'em when he took a bit of pie into the master. Mrs. Ledbetter said as how his lordship was alone with you at his inn, he ruined you and is honorbound to marry you now. Your da is going to call on him tomorrow. Oh, miss, whatever will you do?"

Thinking very uncharitable thoughts about her companion, Gillian raised her chin. "Even in England, they cannot force a girl to marry someone she does not wish to."

"No, miss, but if word gets about, and you may be sure it will, no one else will have you, either. It's no choice you have."

"We shall see about that," Gillian declared, her eyes glinting with anger.

Lucy looked doubtfully at her. "What will you do, miss?"

"I don't know yet, but I shall think of something," Gillian replied as she rose and crossed to stand before the fire. She rubbed her hands briskly and complained, "Is it always so dreadfully cold here? I vow 'tis little wonder I cannot think clearly." Without giving the maid a chance to reply, she turned toward the windows overlooking the square. "A pity I cannot see Lord Wrexham before Papa does. If only I could talk to him . . ."

"Let me fetch you a cup of hot chocolate, miss. It will warm you and—"

Gillian shook her head. "Thank you, but no. I fear it will take more than chocolate to restore my spirits. I've made a dreadful mess of things, haven't I? And for Lord Wrexham as well. A fine way to repay him for his kindness—involving him in my problems as though he did not have sufficient of his own to worry him."

Lucy nodded knowingly. "I heard the old lord left him near penniless. Likely to lose the family home. A shame you cannot wed him after all, miss, and then the both of you could get back your homes."

Gillian whirled around. "What did you say?"

Lucy took a step backward. "I'm sorry, miss. I didn't mean anything—"

"No, no," Gillian interrupted. "It was a brilliant idea. Lucy, you have given me the answer!"

"I have?"

"Do you not see? I shall strike a bargain with Lord Wrexham. I shall help him save his home, and then, after I spend a few months here to pacify Papa, his lordship can help me to return to Willowglen. I know I may depend on him—he was exceedingly kind to me. Oh, 'tis a clever notion, indeed. Ours shall be a true marriage of convenience."

Lucy nodded, but her round face reflected her uncertainty. "It sounds grand, miss, only . . ."

"What?" Gillian demanded impatiently. "What could possibly go wrong?"

"I was just thinking, miss, of how you told his lordship you didn't want to marry him. When your papa calls on him, Lord Wrexham will be bound to remember."

"Oh, good heavens, you are right. Dear Lucy, what

would I do without you? I must let Wrexham know at once that I have changed my mind."

"You'll not be slipping out again?" the maid asked, more than a little alarmed.

"No . . . I have not a prayer of getting out this evening, but you can, Lucy, and you must take a letter to his lordship for me. You will do this for me, will you not? I shall be forever in your debt. Now, just a moment while I write to him." She sat down at the desk, her brow wrinkled in concentration as she realized it was no easy task to tell a gentleman that one had changed one's mind and now wished very much to marry him, but only for the purpose of saving one's home. The composition of this missive would take some time.

"Lucy, would you bring me that cup of chocolate after all? I think I shall have need of it."

The maid nodded, stepped out of the room, and softly closed the door. Miss Gillian was like no lady she had ever seen. She seemed such a tiny, helpless little thing, but inside she had a will just like her papa's. Lightning, she was, Lucy thought uncomfortably, and wondered how much ruin would be left in her wake.

Chapter 3

Leo looked with distaste at the foul-smelling tankard Harry sat before him. Merely smelling the vile concoction was sufficient to make him wish he had not indulged so heavily the night before. He glanced up at his friend. "You surely do not expect me to drink this?"

"Trust me," Harry said, drawing up a chair and straddling it. Tall, blond, with boyish good looks and an irreverent sense of humor, he and Leo were like opposite sides of the same coin. Amusement glimmering in his blue eyes, he assured his friend, "This will set you right as a trivet in no time. My man swears by it."

Leo grimaced and lifted the tankard. His head felt as though a dozen members of the Light Brigade had used it for a bridle path. He was willing to try most anything to ease the pain, but just the odor of the strong fumes brought stinging tears to his eyes and a taste of bile to his throat. He sat the steaming tankard down, pushing it across the table. "What the devil is in there?"

Harry grinned. "A glass of mulberry wine, a cup of coffee, and an equal measure of vinegar, heated to boiling, then simmered for five minutes. Guaranteed to clear your head."

"More like to take it off," Leo muttered, then gestured for the serving wench. After he had ordered a cup of black coffee, he turned back to his friend. "Did you ever try this brew yourself?"

"Never found it necessary. I've a harder head than you, but Edwards swears by it."

"Let Edwards drink it, then," Leo replied ungraciously. He regretted allowing his old friend to persuade him to dine at the Guards' Club—regretted the entire evening, although much of it was only a hazy memory. And the part he remembered most clearly, he wished he could forget.

On the way back to his inn, chance had taken him across the Strand toward Covent Garden, and his carriage had passed a gilded barouche he recognized at once. He had only a fleeting glimpse of Diana Beauclerk sitting beside her mother. He knew the carriage belonged to Lord Fenwick, who had the means to offer Diana everything that he, Leo, wished to. The image of her serene blond beauty haunted him. He'd felt so disheartened that he could not face an evening alone and had turned his horses toward St. James. He'd encountered Harry outside White's and allowed his friend to persuade him to share a meal and a bottle at the Guards' Club—only the bottle had turned into a half dozen or so.

He accepted the mug of coffee from the serving wench and inhaled the pungent aroma gratefully. It might not prove as effective as Edwards's cure, but it was certainly more palatable. He took several swallows as he recalled the unjustified tirade he'd endured from Miss Prescott's father. Something else teased at his mind. He dimly recalled leading Harry up to his room . . . and a letter that had been left for him. From the little American? "Wait here," he told Harry. "I shall return in a moment."

Leo took the stairs slowly. His head still felt uncomfortably groggy, and any sudden motion seemed to make it ache alarmingly. His room was a shambles. Harry had not only accompanied him back to the inn but had stayed to finish off another bottle . . . the clothes Leo had worn the evening before littered the floor beside the unmade bed, and dirty glasses stood on the center table. He scanned the room, then saw the envelope he'd recalled, propped on the shaving stand.

The room smelled foul from the leftover wine and stale aroma of tobacco. He pocketed the letter and made his way back to the sitting room. Harry was still at the table, engaged in a flirtatious exchange with a serving girl. Ignoring the pair, Leo settled into his chair and slit open the envelope.

"Later, darling," Harry said, and pinched the girl's shapely bottom as she laughingly turned away. He leaned across the table. "Is that the billet from your little American? You said you thought it was an apology . . . well? What does she have to say?"

"The entire family must be mad . . ."

"Leo! What does she write? You look deuced odd—is Prescott going to call you out?"

"Not . . . not exactly," Leo replied, a dazed look in his gray eyes. "He apparently intends to call on me some-time today."

Harry fired up immediately with the fierce loyalty that made him such a staunch friend. "You needn't fear, old man. I'll stand by you. We'll show this American he's not dealing with just anyone. A pity you don't have your mourning clothes yet—that would impress him—but I—"

"You don't understand, Harry. Prescott has changed his mind. Far from warning me away from his daughter, he has decided I am honor-bound to marry her."

"What? Surely you jest? I thought you said he threat-ened to shoot you if you came near his precious girl?"

"So he did, but that was before he learned I was not only a soldier but also a member of the peerage. Miss Prescott writes that he is now determined I wed her, and she—she begs that I consider the proposition he intends to put before me." Leo shook his head. "I don't understand it. Last night she claimed she came to plead with me *not* to wed her."

"A trap! I see it all," Harry declared, and called for a bottle of brandy. "This is serious, Leo. Obviously the girl set you up—came here with a trumped-up story, played upon your sympathy, and then, when she was certain her father was home, inveigled you into driving her there. No doubt she thinks because you have a title, you're wealthy. She probably—"

"Her father has more money than you and I could ever dream of," Leo interrupted as he continued to read the missive. "She writes that she has realized a marriage between us would be a means of saving both of our homes. Her father is prepared to come down handsomely in the settlements."

"Both your homes?"

"I believe I mentioned Miss Prescott is from Virginia. She wants nothing more than to return there, but her father is insistent that she marry an English gentleman— some sort of promise he made to her mother. She feels that if we were to wed, she would spend a few months here, just long enough to satisfy her father, and then, with my blessing, she could return to her home in America."

Harry poured a generous measure of brandy for each of them and lifted his glass. "It might still be a trick. Are you entirely certain her father is wealthy?"

"I believe so. He's a financier. Dunstone deals with him, and he, under the impression he was doing me a favor, recommended me to Prescott."

Harry whistled. "Dunstone wouldn't steer you wrong— he's been the family's banker for years. Egad, but you've the devil's own luck. I always said you'd an angel on your shoulder. Just when you thought you must lose Farthingale, this falls into your lap. When's the wedding to be?"

Suppressing his annoyance, Leo pushed the brandy away. "You don't think I would actually marry this girl?"

"Don't see why not. I mean, I know it's a bit of a blow to your pride to have to marry a cit's daughter, but, Leo, think of it. You can keep Farthingale. Surely that's worth a small sacrifice on your part?"

Leo stilled. Only the minuscule muscle next to his left eye throbbed. Not even to Harry Fitzjohn, who had grown up on the neighboring estate and who was as close as a brother, would he admit how deeply he cared for his home. Putting Farthingale on the market was the hardest thing he had to bear in his life. It was like having his . . . his soul wrenched from him. The house did not belong to him so much as he belonged to it. He knew others before him in the family had gone to extraordinary lengths to keep the estate intact. He heard again his mother's recriminations, his young sister's heart-wrenching sobs when he'd told them he would be forced to sell . . .

"Leo? I say, old man, I didn't mean to—"

"It's nothing you said, Harry. I simply . . . marriage? It would be under false pretenses. I have nothing to offer Miss Prescott." His eyes darkened as he thought again of Diana Beauclerk. Farthingale might possess his soul, but Diana laid claim to his heart. He knew there was no way he could offer for her now, but he'd cherished a dim hope that someday he might be able to recover the family fortune, and then . . .

"So?" Harry demanded in a gruff voice. He knew well enough what had brought that look of pain to his friend's eyes. He sympathized, but he privately thought Leo better off without Miss Beauclerk. Aloud, he said, "It appears Miss Prescott wants nothing from you but a semblance of a marriage. From what you said, she has her own reasons for wishing this match, and if she is satisfied, why should you cavil? Don't be a fool, Harry. If her

36

father is as rich as you say, you'd be mad not to accept his offer. Think of Farthingale. Think of your sister."

"I have thought of little else," Leo said, fingering the letter in his hand. The lady had obviously written it in a hurry, but it was much like her—rather brash, forthright, and directly to the point. Miss Prescott had never learned the elements of tact, or the more refined art of gentle persuasion that a true lady would employ. Diana, were she in a similar plight, would never have been so bold as to call on him, or to write such a forward letter. She might have told him something of her feelings, but she would have left it to him to come up with a solution. Leo tried to explain something of his feelings to Harry, but his friend would have none of it.

"Good Lord, man, would you rather have a lady trick you into marriage or lay her cards on the table? Personally, I find Miss Prescott's lack of feminine wiles quite refreshing. A pity I don't have a title—I'd offer for the girl myself."

"You haven't met her father yet," Leo warned. "However, I think you are about to have the opportunity. Unless I am much mistaken, Mr. Prescott is without."

They could hear the blustery voice of a man demanding admittance, and the lower but equally insistent tones of the innkeeper doing his best to keep the intruder out. There was no mistaking the American. Although he had not the pronounced soft drawl that marked his daughter's voice, his words were characterized by a loud inflection that was definitely not characteristic of a British gentleman.

The door swung open, and the short, barrel-chested figure of Oliver Prescott barged into the room. "There you are, Lord Wrexham. I must have a word with you."

The innkeeper eyed Leo helplessly. "I am sorry, my lord. I tried to tell the gentleman this was a private parlor, but—"

"Quite all right, Higgins. You may leave us," Leo interrupted as he stood up. "Harry, may I present Mr. Prescott—the gentleman I . . . uh, told you about."

"His lordship mentioned me, did he?" Oliver asked as he strode toward the table, with a hand outstretched. "I'll wager it was not in flattering terms. We had a bit of a dust-up last evening, but it was all a misunderstanding, and I've come personally to offer my apologies."

"How kind of you," Leo murmured.

"Well, now, I hope you ain't the sort of gentleman to hold a father's natural regard for his only daughter against him?" He turned to Harry, adding, "I mistook his lordship for a common soldier. I'm sure you can see how anyone not acquainted with him might do so. Don't believe I caught your name?"

"Sir Harry Fitzjohn," Leo murmured, "but he was just leaving, were you not, Harry?"

"If you wish, but remember what I said, Leo. Think of Farthingale." He nodded to Prescott, then reluctantly left the room, shutting the door behind him.

Leo turned to his guest and gestured toward a chair. "Will you be seated, Mr. Prescott?"

"Well, now, that's almighty kind of you, my lord. Truth is, I half expected you'd try to toss me out on my ear—not that I would be holding it against you if you did. You ask anyone who's done business with me, and they'll tell you Oliver Prescott is a fair-minded man. 'Tis not often I'm wrong, but when I am, I admit it, and I was sure wrong to rake you over the coals."

"Thank you," Leo murmured dryly.

"Of course that's not to say I ain't concerned that you spent a considerable amount of time here alone with my little girl." Shaking his head sadly, he continued, "Now, you and I know it was all innocent-like, but that's not to say folks won't be talking, and when there's talk about a

38

young lady and a gentleman, well, truth is, it's the lady what suffers."

Leo sipped his coffee, silently studying his visitor over the rim. Despite Prescott's bluff, genial manner, Leo was aware of the shrewdness in the narrow-set blue eyes. He also knew that one did not amass a sizable fortune—not even in America—unless one was a tough and capable businessman. It would not do to underestimate Prescott.

"Truth is, my little girl, she's new to London. Folks here don't know her like they do back home, and I'm afraid they won't take it kindly that she called on you all by herself. Now, I know you was just being kind to my girl, but I wish you would've sent her on her way. You receiving her the way you did, and then driving her home, well, sir, I give you the word with no bark on it—it's caused a bit of a problem."

"Indeed?"

"Well, now, you been about Town a bit, my lord. You know what folks are, and I think you know as well as me that they're going to be saying my girl's been ruined." He paused, looking expectantly at Leo.

"What are you suggesting, Mr. Prescott?"

Oliver shook his head, his mouth twisted in a sad frown. "Much as I hate to say it, it 'pears to me that there's only one thing to be done. You, being an honorable man, owe it to my girl to marry her. I should hate for the papers to publish that Lord Wrexham compromised my girl, then refused to do right by her."

"And I should hate being inveigled into such a position." Leo rose to his feet and paced the room. After a moment he turned and faced Prescott. "Odd that such concern for your daughter was not in evidence last evening. As I recall, far from wishing that I wed her, you ordered me to never come near her again."

Prescott chuckled. "You got me there, my lad. Fact is, if I had known who you was then, I would've invited you

39

in, and we could've settled matters between us fair and square."

Leo stared at him in disbelief. "Is my title all that matters to you, sir? Would you marry your daughter off to any member of the peerage who is willing?"

The genial look fled Prescott's face, and his eyes narrowed to hard slits. "Don't be mistaking me, my lord. My girl means the world and all to me, and I'll be seeing her properly cared for. I know who you are, who your parents, your grandparents, and your great-grandparents are. I know every parcel of land you own, and how much you stand in debt to the last sixpence. I know all about that place you call Farthingale and how much blunt you'll need to set it to rights. I know you have a young sister that you are responsible for, and a mother who never learned to economize. I know who your friends are, who your banker is, and every detail of your military career. I know you don't drink to excess, and I know you ain't given over to gaming. The word is you're an honorable man or I wouldn't be sparing the breath to speak to you."

Stunned by the extent of Prescott's knowledge, and more than a little annoyed that his personal affairs had been so openly discussed, Leo snapped, "You've learned a great deal in a very short time."

Oliver barked a harsh laugh. "Truth is, I can buy and sell a dozen like you, my lord, no offense intended."

"And you think you can buy me for your daughter?" Leo shot back.

"I wouldn't be putting it that way. Come now, my lord. We can deal together, you and I, and both of us will be the better for it. You do right by my girl, and you won't ever have to worry over the ready again. You can buy up the mortgages on Farthingale and launch your sister proper-like. You'll be able to take care of your ma and settle all your debts. You've my word on it, and there's

40

none that can say Oliver Prescott's word ain't as solid as gold."

Leo sighed and ran a hand through his dark curls. It was useless to let anger ride him. This man had not the least idea of how offensive he was. Controlling his temper with an effort, he tried another tact. "What of your daughter, sir? Suppose Miss Prescott and I do not suit?"

A glimmer of amusement crinkled Oliver's blue eyes, and his wide mouth turned up in a grin as he looked Wrexham over. "Not suit? Well, if you don't, I'll wager it would be your own fault, my lord. You cut a fine figure, and from what I've learned, you're a favorite with the ladies. Seems to me, you could turn my girl up sweet if you've a mind to."

"You flatter me, Mr. Prescott. But if you are expecting a love match, I must tell you that my affections are engaged elsewhere."

"Miss Beauclerk, eh? Nay, lad, don't glare at me. I told you I knew about you, and I know the two of you was sweet on each other, but the lady is above your touch now. 'Pears to me the best thing you can do is marry well and make the best of what's been handed you."

"The advantage would appear to be all mine," Leo replied, sarcasm tingeing his words. "But what of your daughter, sir? Do you truly wish her to make a marriage of convenience? Have you no regard for what her feelings must be?"

For the first time since he'd entered the room, Oliver looked defeated. He slumped in his seat and raised weary eyes to meet Leo's gaze. "Mayhap, when you're a father, you'll understand my feelings. Gillian's had the chance to marry where she will and whistled down the wind a dozen offers. I promised her ma I'd see her proper wed, and like I said, my lord, I keep my word. 'Tis time my girl married. Course, that ain't to say that if she was to

41

take you in dislike, I'd be forcing her. What I had in mind was that you come to supper. Take her and that companion of hers driving and out to the theater and such. Then, if all goes well, we'll be posting the banns."

"Mr. Prescott, I cannot—"

"Now, don't be hasty, my lord. For now, all I'm asking is that you come to supper. What do you say?"

Leo smiled wryly. "It appears I have little choice. What evening did you have in mind?"

"Why, this evening, my lord. There's no time to be lost."

"Ah, that must be his lordship now," Mrs. Ledbetter said as she caught the sound of carriage wheels in the square. She rose and smoothed the satin skirt of her gown. "Gillian, my dear, remember what I told you."

Behind the lady's back, Gillian sighed. Her companion had spent the day giving her much advice about captivating a gentleman, most of which seemed impossibly foolish. Listen raptly to whatever he has to say . . . laugh at any witticisms he may utter . . . express one's admiration that he is so clever . . . Mrs. Ledbetter's list went on and on. But what if he is not clever or witty, Gillian had ventured to ask, and received a scold in return. Mrs. Ledbetter held that the truth did not matter in the least. Gentlemen, she insisted, had such enormous egos that any flattery, no matter how outrageous, was certain to be well received.

Gillian retained her doubts, especially in regard to Lord Wrexham, whom she guessed to be of more than moderate intelligence. *He* would not be taken in by such blatant flattery. Nervously she pleated the folds of her skirt. She wished again that her father had not invited him to dine so soon . . . her palms were damp. She looked up as the door opened and Broom announced his lordship.

She watched her father step forward, his voice sounding

unnaturally loud and hearty when measured against Lord Wrexham's cool response. Her chest suddenly felt too tight to breathe, her mouth too dry to speak. Wishing she could somehow disappear, Gillian sought vainly for an excuse to flee the room. But it was too late. Her father was leading Wrexham across the room to her.

Mechanically she lifted her hand and found the courage to raise her head to meet his gaze. His eyes were as gray and cold as the winter sky before the first snowfall.

"A pleasure to see you again, Miss Prescott," he murmured smoothly.

She knew there wasn't an ounce of truth in his words. This was not the kind, understanding soldier she'd spoken with the evening before. This gentleman was every inch a lord, from the folds of the snow-white cravat at his throat to the sheen of his polished black shoes with the jeweled buckles. In his tailored mourning clothes, he looked as regal and unapproachable as a king. Lordy, they had nothing like him in Virginia. What had she done?

Mrs. Ledbetter tittered. "You shall have to excuse Miss Prescott, my lord. She is a trifle shy in company. But there, I am sure we are all aware of the honor you do us, particularly at this trying time in your life. You must allow me to offer my condolences. Your father and brother were both fine gentlemen and shall be greatly missed."

Wrexham turned his attention to her companion, and Gillian was able to breathe again. She watched him discreetly, wishing that he had worn his uniform with the frayed sleeves and faded color. . . .

"My dear, do you not agree?" Mrs. Ledbetter asked suddenly.

Caught daydreaming, Gillian flushed.

Lord Wrexham glanced in her direction, and a little of

43

the iciness of his expression thawed. He couldn't help feeling a trifle sorry for the girl. The unbecoming rush of color to her face turned it a bright red, clashing horribly with the tightly crimped curls bunched about her brow and ears. Aloud, he said, "I cannot say I agree with Mrs. Ledbetter. Personally, I find Town life rather tedious, but I believe this is your first Season. Surely you have not been in London sufficiently long to grow tired of all the balls?"

Gillian's color receded, and her gratitude at his rescue showed in her eyes. "A month, my lord, though it seems much longer."

"My dear, you shall have his lordship thinking you dislike attending balls," said Mrs. Ledbetter.

"I do," Gillian replied uncompromisingly.

"You liked them well enough at home," her father pointed out, and to Wrexham added, "Of course, she knew everyone there. It's not the same here, with my girl not knowing her way about. But I expect it'd be different were she to attend one of those fancy balls with someone like you for an escort. She'd be on the dance floor soon enough then, and the truth is, there's few as graceful as my little girl."

Oh, Papa, don't, Gillian silently pleaded, wishing her father's fondness for her would not lead him into pushing her forward so blatantly. She saw Lord Wrexham stiffen again.

"I am sorry to disappoint you, Mr. Prescott, but as you undoubtedly know, I was wounded on the Peninsula and remain a trifle lame. I am unable to dance."

Oliver Prescott was, for once, dumbfounded, and Mrs. Ledbetter left speechless. Gillian found her voice and suggested softly, "We should not keep you standing, then. Pray be seated, my lord, and may we offer you a glass of . . . of sherry, or perhaps brandy?"

Leo turned and was not proof against the entreaty in her eyes. He smiled slightly. "No mint juleps?"

Surprised, Gillian laughed. "I regret not, but Papa tells me the Bordeaux he has acquired is tolerable."

"Tolerable? 'Tis more than that!" Oliver declared, and regaled his lordship with a lengthy tale of how he came by a case of the smuggled wine. As he spoke, he crossed to the sideboard and poured out two glasses. "I don't mind owning, this lot cost me a pretty penny, but I don't begrudge it. You be the judge, my lord."

Leo took a cautious sip and was pleasantly surprised. He would not have expected Prescott to be a wine connoisseur, but the Bordeaux was exceptional—far superior to the vintage that Harry had supplied the night before. "You are right, Mr. Prescott, 'tis excellent."

"Well, drink up, my lord. There's plenty where that came from, and I've reserved another for our supper that I've a liking for. You needn't fear you'll find any watered-down wine at Oliver Prescott's table."

Lord Wrexham, taxing his mind for a civil reply, was saved the effort as Broom threw open the doors of the drawing room and announced supper.

Prescott poked his guest lightly in the ribs. "After you, my lord. You and Gillian lead the way, and I'll follow with Mrs. Ledbetter here. Might as well get used to having my little girl on your arm, eh?"

The sound of her father's hearty laughter ringing in her ears, Gillian allowed Wrexham to escort her down the gracefully curving Adam staircase and through the long hall. She was blushing again, the betraying rush of color sweeping over her face and shoulders. Her hand, resting against his lordship's sleeve, trembled slightly.

Leo, seeking to set her at ease, said softly, "Your father is certainly an original, Miss Prescott. I do not believe I have ever encountered another quite like him."

Gillian, who had frequently bemoaned her father's

45

lack of sensibility, nevertheless resented anyone else criticizing him. Her chin lifted, and her wide blue eyes shot
sparks of indignation. "Papa may not be a gentleman by
London standards, but he is kind and thoughtful, and in
his own way, he is trying to set you at ease, my lord."

Surprised, Leo glanced down at her. She was almost
pretty in her anger. He patted her hand. "I assure you, I
meant no offense. I can see that you are most fond
of him."

"I love him dearly," Gillian replied stoutly. "And
except for this notion that I must wed an English gentleman, he has never denied me anything. Papa is exceedingly generous, and wishes only for my happiness."

"One can assuredly see that."

"Thank you." Mollified, and irrepressibly honest, she
added in a voice that perfectly mimicked her father's,
"Truth is, he drives me mad."

Chapter 4

Supper was not the ordeal Gillian had imagined it would be. Lord Wrexham was polite to Mrs. Ledbetter without being condescending. He listened to Gillian's opinions with flattering attention and laughed at her small efforts at wit so appreciatively she could almost believe he was content to be dining with her instead of with his friends. He even drew her father out, discussing with him the wisdom of investing heavily on the exchanges. Gillian watched them with a measure of contentment.

Her papa might not be at ease in an elegant drawing room, but no man was shrewder when it came to business, and she was pleased to see that Lord Wrexham listened to him with an air of respect. Only one uncomfortable moment occurred when Oliver Prescott leaned back in his chair and pronounced, "A pity about your father, my lord."

Wrexham nodded politely. "He shall be greatly missed."

"Well, that, too, of course, but what I meant was it's a pity he didn't listen to his banker. I know for a fact Dunstone advised him against investing in that mine that cost him a bundle."

"Perhaps so, sir, but it was not the first time my father acted against his banker's advice. In the past he was most successful, and even Dunstone said that had he lived longer, he might have recouped the family fortune."

"I doubt it. Odds were against him. That's the difference between me and your father. I invest where the odds are in my favor—your pa was ruled by emotion and impulse. Sooner or later, he had to crash. Now you have a pretty sharp man in Halthorpe. Me and him can deal together and if—"

"I beg your pardon," Leo interrupted. He sat down his glass and with chilly civility asked, "Do I understand you to say that you have spoken with my man of business?"

Surprised, Oliver stared at him. "Do you think I would not investigate the gentleman I'm proposing to hand over a tidy fortune to, not to mention my daughter? Of course I talked with your man—as I had with Dunstone. Talked with a score of others, too. But you needn't be thinking they were acting against your interests, my lord. Every single one of them is anxious to see you come about—"

Mrs. Ledbetter tried to intervene. "Really, Mr. Prescott, I hardly think this is the proper time to be discussing such matters."

Oliver might have dismissed her opinion as unimportant, but he noticed Gillian's stricken look and his lordship's icy demeanor. With unaccustomed humility, he owned, "Put my foot in my mouth, haven't I? Truth is, I ain't much in the way of sitting down to dine with lords. Gillian, you tell his lordship here about that play you went to see, and I'll just button my lip."

The moment passed, but Gillian was aware that his lordship was no longer at ease. Her own embarrassment increased as Mrs. Ledbetter recounted a list of notable personages they'd seen at the theater—making it sound as though they had actually spoken to the Duke of Norfolk or Lady Jersey instead of merely noting their presence from across the room. She sighed, counting the moments until the ladies could withdraw. But even that brief respite was denied her.

As she rose, her father stood also. "Gillian, you take his lordship up and show him the picture gallery. I want a word with Mrs. Ledbetter here. We'll join you in a few moments."

"But, Papa—"

"Really, Mr. Prescott, can we not—"

"Females!" Oliver boomed in exasperation and turned to Wrexham. "Whoever said a man was king of his castle never lived with a passel of women. They'll argue morning till dusk over the simplest matter. Now, my lord, you have no objection to seeing the gallery, do you?"

"None at all, sir," Leo said, smiling gently at Gillian, but she had her head bent and did not see. He crossed around to her side and murmured, "I should be honored if you would show me the picture gallery."

"This way, my lord," she replied, without looking at him. She silently led him up the steps, past the drawing room, and into the long hall.

Leo had seen dozens of picture galleries. Nearly every home of note had one, and many measured their success by the possession of a portrait painted by the latest artist to come into favor. At the moment it was Lawrence, and before that Sir Joshua Reynolds or Hogarth. His own portrait had been painted by Reynolds several years ago and hung in the long gallery at Farthingale. He expected to see a similar display here—not of the Prescotts' ancestors, for the house had been let furnished, but of the previous owners. He glanced at the first small panel positioned near eye level on his right and drew in his breath.

"Exquisite . . . but this looks remarkably like a Rembrandt. . . ." He drew closer and examined it more carefully.

"It is," Gillian informed him. "Papa calls it *The Bridge*, and it is one of his favorite pieces. There is another by Rembrandt farther along—that one is larger, a portrait of a Jewish priest, a rabbi I believe. It was painted sometime in the early sixteen hundreds. Papa says you can see the man's soul in his eyes. It is one of the few portraits he owns. He prefers the landscapes. . . ." She moved on, describing in a rather mechanical voice the various oils mixed with pastels, the details of when the art was rendered and by whom.

Leo strolled beside her, barely able to take in the enormous beauty of all he saw. His mind reeling, he asked, "But surely these were not left in the house?"

"Oh, no. They are Papa's private collection. Paintings are his one passion, and he would not leave them behind in Virginia or put them in storage here. 'Tis one of the reasons he chose this house. Although it was let furnished, the gallery was nearly empty. The few paintings that were left, he put in the attic."

Leo turned to look down the long hall again. "Remarkable."

"Do you think so, my lord? I confess I find them pretty to look at, but I do not share Papa's enthusiasm. Sometimes I think he would sell everything he owns in order to buy just one more. When he was in France last year, he saw a painting by Jean-Honoré Fragonard called *The Bathers*, which he much coveted, but the owner would not sell it. Papa offered an enormous sum and was downcast for weeks when he could not acquire it. I believe he means to try again while we are in England."

"Your father has excellent taste, Miss Prescott."

She heard the surprise in his voice, but did not wonder at it. "Perhaps we should rejoin Papa now," she said.

"If you like, but I am glad your father thought to provide us with a few moments alone. I received your letter. . . ."

She turned away from him, blushing furiously once again. "I know it was presumptuous of me to write you so."

"You must not think that, but I confess I am curious as to what changed your mind," he said gently. "When we spoke last night, you were much against this scheme. Will you tell me honestly, is this marriage truly what you desire, or have you agreed merely because it is what your father wishes?"

She stood facing the door but was very aware of his presence just behind her. She inhaled, breathing in the scent of him that reminded her of the woods on a spring morning. It was difficult to think with him standing so close. She bit her lip to concentrate, then finally replied, "I confess I disliked the notion when Papa first proposed it, but once I met you, I . . . I realized we might contrive well together. If you agree that I can return to Willowglen after a few months, I think a . . . a marriage of convenience may prove an ideal solution for both of us. . . ."

He had to lean forward to catch her words, so softly were they spoken. He knew she had no idea of the enormity of what she was proposing, and she had no mother or other female to advise her. . . .

"Of course, if you dislike the notion, or feel we would not suit, I quite understand," she added, a catch in her voice.

"My dear, 'tis not so much that I dislike the idea—indeed, I can see only myriad advantages for me—but I do think that perhaps you have not thought this through carefully. I have certain concerns that I think we should discuss." He lifted a hand to her shoulder and gently turned her to face him.

Gillian shivered at his touch. It was not an unpleasant sensation and did not arise out of fear. Startled by her body's reaction, she resisted a sudden and strong temptation to step into the warmth of his arms. Retreating a step

51

so that her back was pressed against the door, she asked, "Concerns?"

"There is more to marriage—even a marriage of convenience—than having the banns called or exchanging vows," he began, but hesitated as he saw the hurt look in her eyes.

"You need not fear that I would be living in your pocket, my lord," she said bravely, only the slight trembling of her chin betraying her emotion. With one hand behind her, she managed to wrench open the door. She turned quickly and slipped through, tossing words back over her shoulder, "Indeed, from what I have observed, I gather it is the custom of many husbands and wives to live quite apart. You may be assured that I will not hang on your sleeve."

He knew how much it must have cost her to make that admission, and swore silently. She had taken his words wrong. The girl was like Harry—leaping to conclusions and embarking on harebrained schemes without thinking of the consequences. Wondering what the devil he was supposed to do now, he followed her out into the hall and caught up with her just as she entered the drawing room.

Oliver Prescott and Mrs. Ledbetter were waiting for them. Gillian crossed to the sofa, seated herself, and became immediately engrossed in pouring out a cup of tea and fussing with the cups. She looked, Leo thought, like a pixie. Amused by his own whimsical thoughts, he turned away. Absurd to imagine Miss Prescott in such a light. She had more practicality and courage than a dozen young ladies he knew. Pixie, indeed.

"Well, my lord, what did you think of my pictures?" Oliver asked, clapping his guest on the shoulder. His manner was as bluff and hearty as usual, but a hint of uncertainty had crept into his voice.

Leo smiled, able to reply with perfect sincerity, "I feel

privileged to have viewed them, sir, and I hope you will allow me to come again when I've more time. Seldom have I seen such a remarkable collection. Have you someone who advises you on your purchases?"

Oliver beamed. "Nay, my lord. I buy what appeals to me. There's a tidy fortune tied up in that gallery, I don't mind telling you. Some of those paintings I've had for years, and they're worth ten times again what I paid for them. Now then, tell me which one appealed to you most."

Leo accepted a cup of tea from Miss Prescott's hand and answered unhesitatingly, "*The Talbot.*" He had been moved by the small but exquisite landscape of rolling hills and winding river rendered by an American artist. Something of the wild beauty of the setting reminded him of Farthingale.

"You would not be trying to turn me up sweet? Did Gillian tell you 'tis one of my favorites?"

"No, sir, but I am not surprised."

"Talbot's not as well known as the others, and doesn't command much of a price yet, but I've a special fondness for that painting. When you tie the knot with my daughter, that shall be one of your wedding presents."

"Papa!" Gillian cried.

"What? Don't be turning missish on me now, girl. And if you're thinking of his lordship, I doubt he minds a little plain speaking. 'Tis what he is here for, after all. Ain't that right, my lord?"

Uncertain of what he was being asked to agree to, Leo gestured helplessly. "You are very generous, Mr. Prescott, but neither your daughter nor I have come to an agreement as yet. I think we both need more time to—"

"Time?" Oliver thundered. "You haven't any to spare, my lord. Don't you know that your affairs are in such a tangle that unless we act at once, it might be too late to save that house of yours?"

"Even if it means losing Farthingale, you must grant me a day or two in which to come to a decision," Leo replied. His tone remained civil, but firm. One could not doubt he meant precisely what he said.

Oliver opened his mouth, then shut it again, plainly at a loss for words. He was not in the habit of having his wishes, which were generally interpreted as orders, ignored.

Leo, correctly reading the confusion in his host's eyes, hid a smile before turning to Gillian with a small bow. "I believe it would benefit us both to spend some time together, Miss Prescott. Will you do me the honor of driving out with me on the morrow? If you are agreeable, I shall call for you at four."

"I think you look very nice, miss," Lucy remarked late on Friday afternoon as her mistress studied her reflection in the long looking glass.

"I suppose it will have to do," Gillian replied unhappily. She pushed one of the tightly curled tresses off her brow, the better to examine her features. Her blue eyes were easily the best. She did not squint like that unfortunate girl at Mrs. Dunstone's, or have eyes that crossed, but she did wish her lashes were darker and the curving brows above not mixed with the same red-gold strands that colored her hair. But she couldn't do anything about that or change her regrettably short nose sprinkled with an abundance of freckles. Even had she heeded the advice of a dozen governesses and worn a protective bonnet while out riding, it would not alter the short upward tilt of her nose into the long aquiline shape that marked a true beauty . . . but she was honest enough to own that it might have protected her skin from all those freckles. She had tried dusting her face with rice powder, but that made her look like a ghost.

She frowned, then quickly composed her mouth into a

straight line. Taken alone, her lips were not ill-shaped, but the whole was, she felt, too large for her face. She must remember not to smile, or frown, for to do either made her mouth look even larger.

"Is it to be this one, then, miss, or the yellow?"

Gillian stepped back to observe the full effect of the pomona green walking dress that had been delivered that morning. The result was disappointing. When she'd seen it illustrated in a fashion plate, it had looked most attractive and extremely modish, but on her it looked no better than the dozen of other dresses she'd tried on. She thought that particular shade ill became her, but both Mrs. Ledbetter and the modiste had assured her it was the latest fashion. If only she were taller . . . the high waist-line and the ruffled bodice seemed to emphasize her short stature.

"His lordship will be here soon," Lucy tactfully reminded her.

Gillian glanced at the mantel clock. She still had twenty minutes to the hour—twenty minutes to wish for a miracle to transform her into a beauty. Might as well wish for the moon, she thought. And what did it matter, after all? She reminded herself that Lord Wrexham was not courting her. Their marriage, if it came to be, would be one of convenience—which was precisely what she herself wanted. Only . . . he was very kind, and she did not wish him to be embarrassed if they chanced to meet his friends while out driving . . . or to be pitied.

She turned away from the mirror and instructed her maid, "Fetch my straw hat with the green ostrich feathers, and see if you can find my gloves."

The bonnet proved a fortunate choice. It hid most of her tightly crimped curls and the tall curving brim provided a few additional inches to her height. Gillian surveyed the effect. She might never be a beauty, but at least she did not look like a complete dowd. She swept up her gloves and her reticule just as her father's voice bellowed up the stairs.

"Gillian! His lordship is here. Hurry up, now, girl, you don't wish to keep him waiting."

She rushed out into the hall, leaned over the banister, and called, "Coming, Papa." If she did not acknowledge him, he would continue shouting. Though Gillian had remonstrated with him, he still held that it was foolish to send a servant up for her when he could as easily raise his voice.

She drew in a deep breath, stiffened her back, and lifted her chin. Head up, she descended the winding staircase in what she hoped was an elegant, poised manner. Lord Wrexham and her father awaited her in the hall below. Gillian resolutely kept her eyes fixed straight ahead, using one hand on the banister to guide her slow steps. She'd practiced a greeting and as she neared the bottom, she said with tolerable composure, "Good day, Lord Wrexham. It would appear we have lovely weather for a—"

Her words were abruptly cut off as the heel of her half boot caught in the hem of her walking dress. Her hand slipped off the railing. She lost her footing, and with a small, helpless cry, pitched forward.

Wrexham, with the lightning reflexes that had won him so many honors and saved his skin on the battlefield, moved before her father even realized the danger. He easily caught her in his arms. She was as light as a feather pillow, but his knee could not bear the sudden exertion and collapsed beneath him. He landed with a thud against the bottom step, Miss Prescott in his lap. She was a tangle of arms and legs, silken skirts, and feathers that tickled his nose.

Mortified, her bonnet knocked askew, Gillian struggled to rise.

"Are you hurt?" he asked as he helped her to her feet.

"No . . . thank you," she murmured, her face flaming. She could not face him and muttered, "Pray, excuse me for a moment while I fix my hat," and fled into the drawing room.

"Don't be worrying about my girl," Oliver said, half inclined to laugh. "It ain't the first tumble she's taken, and likely won't be the last. Never saw such a girl for falling down. But what of you, my lord? You ain't hurt, are you?"

"Only my dignity. This knee of mine gives way at the most inopportune times."

"Perhaps you'd like to come in and have a spot of brandy to set you right?" Oliver gestured toward the drawing room.

"Thank you, sir, but I have my carriage out front, and I dislike keeping my horses standing. If Miss Prescott is not hurt . . ."

Her hat righted, her color still high, Gillian emerged from the drawing room as he spoke. "I am fine, my lord, and ready to leave if you are." She stood on tiptoe and kissed her father's cheek, then swept toward the door as Broom opened it.

They walked out in silence, both at a loss for words, and then both spoke at once.

"I must apologize, my lord, for—"

"I am sorry, Miss Prescott, that I—"

Their laughter mingled in the cool afternoon air. Lord Wrexham helped her into his carriage, nodded to his tiger to release his horses, then gave his team of chestnuts the signal to start. When they were firmly under control, he turned to her with a smile. "Pray, don't apologize. 'Tis not often a gentleman is fortunate enough to have a lovely young lady fall into his arms. I only regret that I made such a muff of it by dropping you."

Gillian looked away from him. She vaguely noticed Lady Carlisle leaning out her window as they left the

57

square, and several other neighbors turning to stare after the carriage. Under different circumstances, she might have taken pleasure in their astonishment at seeing her drive out with such a distinguished gentleman. She knew what they said of her. She had few illusions about herself—something Lord Wrexham needed to learn.

She stared at the horses before her and said in a low voice, "You need not trouble yourself to flatter me, my lord. If we are to deal together successfully, there should be no pretense between us."

"I beg your pardon?"

Gillian sighed. "I know that I am not a beauty, so you need not pretend otherwise."

"You are certainly not an antidote. Who has been filling your head with such nonsense?"

"I have eyes in my head, my lord. I am too short, my hair is too red, and . . . and I have freckles."

"I think your freckles charming," Leo said truthfully. "They give you the look of a pixie. As for your being too short, I see I shall have to introduce you to the Duchess of Avalon. She, my dear, is barely as tall as you, but is held to be most alluring. A few years ago she brought the duke, a notorious rake, to heel and has kept him captivated ever since. Come to think of it, her hair is also red. I shall have to be on my guard lest you share her other traits."

"What traits?" she demanded curiously.

"I'm told she has a dreadful temper to match her hair. She used to fence with her brother-in-law and is rumored to be an expert marksman as well."

Gillian laughed. "You need not worry. I have never fired a gun or lifted a sword, and my temper is no worse than any other female's . . . at least, I do not believe it is."

"Then you will not throw a book at my head if I forget an appointment or neglect you overlong?" he teased.

The laughter fled her eyes, and she twisted her gloved

hands in her lap. "I told you, my lord, that I do not intend to hang on your sleeve. You may go your way, and I shall go mine."

"Ah, but that presents a problem, my dear, and it is what I wished to discuss with you," he replied as he guided his horses into the gate at Hyde Park. "I will not pretend that this marriage is the match that I wished to make. However, if we agree to it, then you will be treated in every respect as my wife, with all the care and consideration due her."

Confused, Gillian stared at him. "I am not quite certain I understand you, my lord. Our marriage will be one of convenience only. In a few months, I shall wish to return to Virginia."

"That, uh, may not be possible," Leo replied.

"If you are thinking Papa will disapprove, he very likely will. But once I am married, he can have nothing to say to my conduct. As long as my husband agrees that I may go—why do you look at me so strangely, my lord? You surely cannot object if I leave. You will have your Farthingale, as we agreed."

"Farthingale is the problem," he said as he waved to a couple in a passing carriage. He wished he'd not chosen Hyde Park for this discussion. There were too many other people about, and he could neither rein in, nor give her his full attention.

"I do not understand."

An open landau passed, and the small poodle perched on the seat beside a lady barked furiously. Leo's lead horse shied a little, and he tightened the reins. When the team was under control again, he glanced at Gillian Prescott. Her eyes mirrored the confusion he'd heard in her voice. Searching for the right words, he began haltingly, "Farthingale has been in the Reed family for hundreds of years, passed from one generation to the next. It

59

is unthinkable for it to pass out of our family, or for anyone other than a Reed to inhabit it."

"That much I do understand," she said. "You made that quite clear, and I assume 'tis why you are willing to consider Papa's proposal. Marrying me will save Farthingale for you."

"True, but saving Farthingale would be futile if I cannot leave it to my son. You see, if I do not have an heir, it will pass to a distant relative, and I would as soon sell it as see that happen."

"But you do not have a son . . ." she began, then colored furiously as the full implication of his remarks became clear. "I see. You would expect me to . . . to bear your child?"

She made it sound like the worst fate in the world, Leo thought, and regretted again the necessity that had pitchforked him into this predicament. He would rather face a thousand enemy troops than hear the desolation in her voice. He knew she'd had no idea that such might be expected of her, but he hadn't quite anticipated that she would find the notion so repulsive.

More curtly than he intended, he replied, "I believe it is customary in marriages of convenience for an heir to be secured, especially when there is a title and extensive lands. And I am very certain your father will also be wishful of a grandchild. However, if you are averse to the idea, we may simply tell your father we do not suit, and no more need be said."

When she did not comment, he stole a glance at her. She was sitting stiffly erect and very still—like a little girl unfairly reprimanded. Her face was chalk white, the freckles more pronounced than ever. It was shock, of course, and he cursed himself for not finding a more delicate way of explaining his dilemma.

"I had not considered such a possibility," she remarked suddenly, "but certainly I can see your concern. How extraordinary to think that my son will be the Earl of Wrexham."

"Eventually, but I hope you will not wish to hasten the event," he teased. Relief flooded through him that she was taking this so calmly. "I know this has been something of a shock to you, my dear. Had you a mother or other close female relative to advise you, I would not have broached the subject."

"I am glad you did, my lord. As I said, I wish no pretense between us. But, pray tell me, do you think a year will be sufficient?"

"Sufficient for what?" he asked, not quite certain he had understood her correctly.

"Why, to have your child."

Chapter 5

Leo stared at the diminutive female beside him, unable to believe his ears. Miss Prescott spoke of bearing his child as easily, and with as little concern, as though she were merely discussing the weather.

"Gracious, you have a great many friends, do you not?" she murmured as he absentmindedly returned the wave of an acquaintance.

"Far too many, it would appear," he replied. Hyde Park had been a mistake. He could not talk to her sensibly while controlling his team and returning the salutes of those who hailed him. He had undoubtedly already offended any number of people by giving them the go-by. He racked his brain, trying to think where he might take her. He could not, in good conscience, bring her back to his inn, and to pull up on the road somewhere would leave her prey to the worst sort of scandalbroth. Nor would he find any privacy at her own home—not with her father demanding to know if they'd settled matters between them.

"I believe that gentleman is trying to attract your attention, my lord," she ventured.

Leo glanced to his right and inwardly groaned. Harry was afoot and waving his hat. The earl had no choice but to direct his horses to the side of the drive.

"Thought you meant to give me the cut," his friend said by way of greeting. He stood on Gillian's side of the carriage and grinned up at her, obviously waiting for an introduction.

Regretting the necessity, Leo said, "Miss Prescott, may I present Sir Harry Fitzjohn."

"How do you do?" she responded nervously as she looked down at the gentleman. She had not met any of Lord Wrexham's friends, and she was fearful of saying or doing something that might embarrass him.

"Better now, my dear. Just seeing you has brightened my day considerably—why, I do believe the sun has come out."

She smiled at such nonsense, pointing out, "The sun, sir, has been shining all afternoon."

"Has it, now? And I could've sworn it was a gray cloudy day. Must be that fellow beside you frowning so fiercely. Leo, step down and allow me to tool Miss Prescott once around the park. A walk will do you good—I've seen corpses with better color than you."

"Thank you, Harry," Leo returned dryly. "Very kind of you to be concerned, but if I looked pained, perhaps it is because a most annoying pest keeps flitting around my carriage. Where are you bound for?"

"My aunt has summoned me to tea. I say, Leo, why don't you join us? She probably wants to grill me about you, and she'd enjoy meeting Miss Prescott before the rest of the ton. You know what she's like."

"Tell her you haven't seen me," Leo suggested.

"As if she would believe that!"

"Sorry to be disobliging, but we have other plans. Give Lady Tyndale my regards and assure her I shall bring Miss Prescott to call. Now, step back. I should so hate to run you down."

"Miss Prescott, I appeal to you. Would you not much prefer tea with a charming, elderly lady, who desires nothing so much as to meet you, than driving through the park with a Friday-faced, toplofty peer who thinks—"

"Harry, I am warning you," Leo growled impatiently.

"Oh, very well, have it your way, but I shall expect a full accounting." He laughed, stepped back, then bowed gallantly. "Miss Prescott, your servant."

As Leo snapped the reins and the carriage pulled away, Gillian glanced behind her. She saw the tall, blond young man still standing in the road, grinning irrepressibly. He waved again, and she smiled before turning to her escort and remarking, "Your friend seems most amusing."

"He believes he is, which is what comes of being the only male in a family full of females. He has four older sisters who dote on him and encourage him to think himself a wit, which, I fear, frequently leads him to go beyond line."

"Are you good friends?" she asked curiously.

"We are," Leo answered tersely, for his mind was not on the conversation. He desperately needed to speak with Miss Prescott alone—somewhere without a team of high-strung horses to handle or the likelihood of interruptions from well-meaning friends. The only place he could think of was his town house in Grosvenor Square. He had not opened it on coming down to London because he didn't wish to incur the added expense. At present it was staffed only by the Craddocks, an elderly couple who'd been pensioned off and looked after the house in the family's absence. His home was not an ideal solution. If anyone learned he'd taken Miss Prescott there, it would add weight to her father's claim that she was compromised. Of course that would not matter overmuch if she remained firm in her resolve to marry him.

"I only asked because you seem so different," Miss Prescott said with an air of apology.

"I beg your pardon?"

"You and Sir Harry," she explained. "I only asked if you were friends because you seem so different. I did not mean to pry into your affairs."

"Under the circumstances, you have every right to do so, although I did not take your question in that light. You must forgive me, Miss Prescott. My mind is still preoccupied with the question of our marriage."

"Oh."

They drove in silence for several moments after leaving the park, turning from Park Lane onto Oxford, lined with its neat row of shops.

"May I ask where we are going, my lord?"

"We are nearly there," Leo replied, turning the horses into the familiar brick-laid square. "I hope you do not object, but this is my London home. Only the caretakers are here at present, but I thought we might use the library to continue our discussion."

His tiger jumped down from the rear perch as he halted the carriage and ran around to hold the horses' heads. "Walk them, Jimmy. We shall be some few moments," Leo instructed as he descended, then came to assist Miss Prescott to alight. "I'm afraid the house has been shut up for some time, and you will find it dreadfully dusty, but at least here we may be assured of some privacy."

She said nothing, but allowed him to lead her up to the front door and watched as he unlocked it. They stepped into an immense front hall as bare and empty—and unwelcoming—as a cavern.

"Craddock? Sarah? Is anyone here?" Leo called, his voice seeming to rebound off the walls.

Toward the end of the hall, Gillian saw a door open and an elderly woman, her head wreathed with snow-white hair, peek out. She surveyed them cautiously, then stepped into view. She was thin, terribly thin so that her dress hung loosely on her sparse frame, and her voice, when she raised it, held the quiver that sometimes comes with great age. "Leopold, is that you? Come here, lad, and let me see you."

"Sarah was my nanny," he whispered to Gillian as they

met the old woman halfway. Then he stood still as she looked him up and down. Her eyes glistened, and she reached out a gnarled hand to tentatively touch his sleeve.

"It is you! Gracious, child, how you have grown—but why didn't you tell me you were coming? The house is shut up. We've nothing here to—"

"Don't fret, Sarah," he said in a loud voice. "I'm not staying. I only came by to show Miss Prescott the house. Where is Craddock?"

"Out, and sorry he'll be that he wasn't here to welcome you home, but we weren't never expecting you."

He patted her hand. "It's all right, Sarah. We will be in the library if Craddock returns. Do you understand?"

She nodded, her eyes darting to the young lady and then back to the earl. "Could I make you a cuppa tea?"

"Nothing, thank you, Sarah. Do not disturb yourself. I shall see you again before I leave."

Leo led his guest down the long hall, explaining as they walked, "Sarah has been ill, and she is near deaf, so 'tis difficult to explain anything to her. She and her husband mostly live in the kitchen, and keep an eye on the house." He paused before a pair of double doors and threw one open, gesturing to Gillian to enter.

She stepped in and halted. The library had the dank, fusty odor of rooms too long shut up. In the darkness she could see only large white-sheeted shapes that loomed before her like ghostly figures.

"I had forgot how forbidding this room can be," Leo said, reaching for a candelabra. He lit several of the candles, then handed it to her. "Hold this for a moment if you will."

She watched him whisk the Holland covers from two tall wing chairs, then push a small center table between them. "There, that is better, is it not?" he asked, turning to smile at her.

Gillian longed for the warmth of the afternoon sun, but she agreed it was certainly an improvement. She took the seat he offered, setting the branch of candles down on the table. The flames flickered, casting shadows that only seemed to emphasize the vastness of the room. She could not even see into the corners.

"Rather cozy, what?" Leo said as he sat down opposite her. "I am sorry I cannot offer you a fire, but we shall not remain here long. You are not too cold, are you?"

Her walking dress was thin, and she could feel a draft swirling around her shoulders. She nevertheless managed a smile and said, "Not at all, my lord, but I do not understand why you have brought me here."

"To talk about our proposed marriage," he replied earnestly as he leaned forward in his chair. "We could not discuss it properly in the park, and I did not want to take you home again until we had settled matters. Your father is most anxious on that head."

The candlelight lit his face, and she could see how serious and troubled his gray eyes were. Her own, she knew, must mirror her confusion. "I am afraid I still do not see . . ."

"Miss Prescott, I—" He stopped and sighed. "Perhaps, under the circumstances, you will grant me leave to address you informally?"

"Certainly, my lord."

"My friends call me Leo," he told her, then rose to his feet. He was too restless, too much at a loss for words to remain seated. He paced the room for a moment, then halted and knelt before her chair. "Gillian, I must be certain you understand what you are agreeing to. When you asked me if I thought a year sufficient, what precisely did you mean?"

"It seems very simple to me, my lord. You require a son to inherit Farthingale. I shall do my best to provide you with one, after which I shall be free to return to

America. The only difficulty is that I am not entirely sure how long it may take to ... to become with child." Knowing she was blushing furiously, she was devoutly thankful for both the candlelight and the privacy of the room.

He reached for one of her hands and took it in his own. "Do you ... are you aware of what is involved ... that is, do you know how a lady becomes enceinte?" he asked, using the popular French term.

Her lashes swept down, hiding her eyes. "I do not know the details, of course. My neighbor's daughter became large with child not long after she wed, and one of our maids ... she said a gentleman seduced her and Papa turned her off. She was rather witless and less than capable, so surely it cannot be so very difficult a thing?"

His head sank to his chest as he closed his eyes for a moment, not knowing whether to laugh at her innocence or sob in frustration. He only knew he could not take advantage of it. And there remained her naive assumption that once she'd given birth, she could easily leave the child. He knew her own mother had died when she was very young, so perhaps she did not understand the bond that formed between a woman and a child ... or perhaps she was one of those females who lacked the maternal instinct ...

"Leo?" she said hesitantly.

He lifted his head and gazed up into a pair of wide blue eyes regarding him with concern. "Gillian, my dear, I don't believe you understand how difficult it would be to leave your own child."

"Well, naturally I realize that parents grow most fond of their children over time, but if I leave at once—before I've time to become attached? And 'tis not as though I would be abandoning the child." She smiled sweetly down at him. "I may not know you well, but I am entirely certain you would take excellent care of your son."

"Of course I would, but—"

"I have been thinking, and although it will be somewhat inconvenient and delay my return to Willowglen, I am glad you feel so strongly that we should have a child."

"You are?"

"Oh, yes. It occurs to me that Papa will not be at all pleased when I leave, but if he has a grandson, that will certainly console him. I hope you will not mind too much, Leo, but Papa will take a great interest in the child—have you considered a name for the boy?"

"Not yet," he replied unsteadily. He rose to his feet, drawing Gillian up with him. "And there is no guarantee that your first child will be a boy."

"I had not thought of that. Is there nothing we can do to make certain?"

"No, my dear. We cannot even be certain that you will conceive immediately. All we can do is try."

He'd retained her hands in his and was standing very close. Something in his voice and the tender way he gazed at her made Gillian suddenly shy of him. She was acutely aware of his presence, acutely aware that they were virtually alone in the house. "My lord, I—"

"Leo," he corrected softly, and drew her still closer. "My dear, do you have the slightest idea of how a child is conceived?"

"Only that it . . . it involves an intimacy between a husband and wife," she murmured, so low he could barely hear her words. Her drawl was more pronounced, and her small hands trembled between his.

"It begins with kisses," he explained. He brought one of his hands up beneath her chin and lifted her face toward his. "There is a great deal more, but for now we shall simply discover if you find my kisses distasteful. Has any gentleman ever kissed you, Gillian?"

69

"Besides Papa, do you mean? Only . . . once," she admitted, unable to tear her gaze from his.

"And did you enjoy it?"

"No . . . he'd had too much to drink and smelled of spirits . . ."

"I trust I don't," Leo said, and dropped a featherlight kiss on her brow where a tiny vein throbbed. "Don't be afraid, my dear. I would do nothing to hurt you."

Her eyes swept shut as he released her hand, then reached around her waist to draw her close against his chest. She could hear his heart beating and wondered if he could hear the wild pounding of her own heart—but it was not from fear. Without knowing why, she trusted him implicitly. Then his lips were touching the corner of her mouth, still light as butterflies . . . she felt the same sensation she'd experienced in the gallery. As naturally as though she had done it a thousand times, Gillian lifted her arms around his neck.

Slowly, Leo warmed himself as she willingly accepted his embrace. He kissed her, gently at first, just touching her lips with the tip of his tongue. When she responded, he deepened the kiss, and was surprised by the sudden surge of desire he felt. Abruptly, he released her and stepped back.

Gillian opened her eyes and blinked at him. It was as though the sun had suddenly passed behind a cloud, depriving her of a welcome warmth. "That was not . . . not at all like Freddy. . . ."

"Well, that answers one question at least," Leo responded with a chuckle. "I do not think you will find this business of conceiving a child unbearable."

"Have you seduced me, then?"

"Good Lord, no! Gillian, you must not go about saying such a thing. I have only kissed you, and kissing is merely a prelude to seduction. There is more—a great deal more—but that shall have to wait until we are properly wed."

Her mind teasing her with tantalizing thoughts of what might follow, Gillian merely nodded. Then, realizing the import of his words, she whispered, "Does that mean you are agreeable to our marriage?"

"If you are, my dear. I still have reservations and fear you may find it very different from what you imagine, but yes, I am quite willing."

"And you will not object if I wish to return to America after we . . . we have a child?"

"I still think you may change your mind—indeed, I hope you will—but you have my word that if you still wish to go, I will not object. And now, I think I had best take you home."

"Leo?"

Her voice was a mere whisper, drawing out his name in a soft cadence of vowels. He could hear both a plea and a hesitancy in that one word. Gently he took her hand and asked, "What is it, my dear?"

"Would you mind very much . . . that is, just so I may remember what 'tis like . . . would you kiss me once more before we go?"

Leo had a late supper at White's with Harry. They occupied a small table situated in one corner of the coffee room, between the fireplace and the double doors that led into the hall. The night was fairly warm, so the fire was not laid, but the room was amply lit by the glow of candles in two large chandeliers and the single tapers that stood on each of the tables atop a glistening white cloth. The position of their table afforded them the opportunity to see who came and went, and to observe the other members of the exclusive club. But this evening neither gentleman stirred, nor looked about, except to call for more wine.

Leo, recounting some of the less intimate details of his conversation with Gillian Prescott, confided, "She has no more notion than a babe of what is involved. I should be court-martialed for taking advantage of her, and instead her father hands her to me on a silver platter—no, make that gold. Oliver Prescott would not use anything so mundane as mere silver."

Harry laughed at his friend's woebegone expression. "Come out of the mopes, old man. It appears to me you've struck an excellent bargain. A willing bride with a wealthy father anxious to fork over the dibs in style—for what more could a gentleman ask?"

"When you are better acquainted with my future father-in-law, then you may tell me if you are still of that opinion. My own sire may have had his faults, not the least of which was leaving his family in improvident circumstances, but you must own that he was never ostentatious. I wish you might have been present to hear Prescott's plans for the wedding—you will not credit it, but he wished to hire Westminster Abbey for the ceremony and engage the Archbishop of Canterbury to officiate. Why, he even offered to buy the ring I give Gillian!"

Harry's burst of laughter caused the heads of several other gentlemen dining to turn in their direction.

Leo glared at him. " 'Tis all very well for you to laugh, but it was the most provoking interview I have ever endured."

"Leave him to your mother," Harry advised. "She'll peer down her nose at him and soon set him in his place."

"Lord, don't remind me of that meeting—I am dreading the moment. As it is, she will probably swoon when she learns I intend to wed a merchant's daughter." He drank deeply, then sighed. "I must write her this evening and somehow persuade her to come to Town. She'll not wish to do so, but Prescott is insisting I open the town house, at his expense, mind you, and hire an enormous staff."

"How perfectly dreadful of him."

"Do I sound the worst sort of ingrate?" Leo asked ruefully. "The thing is, I know he means well, but he doesn't know where to draw the line. He finds my coachman's livery too tame for his taste, and suggested I change it to scarlet and gold. He even had the cheek to ask if we had sufficient plate and silver to serve the guests. You may laugh, but I tell you there is no bearing it."

Their conversation was suspended for a moment as three gentlemen, all suffering slightly from the effects of several bottles of claret, approached the door. The tallest of the trio, Sir John Tavisham, spotted Leo and hailed him as he staggered toward their table. "Wrexham, I hear congratulations are in order. You sly dog, when is the wedding to be?"

Lord Fordsby, who'd been hanging out for a rich wife for some time, followed in his footsteps and muttered morosely, "Is it true she's an heiress? Stole a march on us . . . 'tis not fair, Wrexham, for you to offer for her before the rest of us have had even a glimpse of the chit. If you were not such an excellent shot, I'd call you out."

Harry snorted impolitely. "Much good it would do you—think any girl would prefer you over Wrexham? Doing it too brown, Fordsby!"

"Is it true, then?" the third member of the trio asked. He was slightly built, possessed of a handsome countenance, marked by dark, brooding eyes and a thin aquiline nose. Not quite as besotted as his friends, he stared at Leo sadly. "I suppose I must offer you my felicitations."

"Egad, Beauclerk, you make it sound more like an occasion for condolences," Harry said before Leo could reply.

"To some of us, so it is. I bid you good evening, gentlemen."

Harry cursed silently. He'd seen the sudden despair in Leo's eyes, and the way the knuckles of his hand turned white as he gripped his wineglass. The meeting had been inevitable, but nevertheless Harry wished Philip Beauclerk had not chosen this night to visit White's. With uncustomary compassion he asked, "Have you seen her since your return?"

Leo shook his head. "I called, of course, but I spoke only with her father. He was very understanding and, I think, regretful, but he thought it would be better if I didn't see Diana. The damnable thing is that I know he is right."

"But you are bound to meet her," Harry objected. "Surely it would be wiser to get it over with, say goodbye properly, and—"

"You don't understand," Leo interrupted. He lifted his glass and drained the last of the wine, then rose to his feet. "Forgive me, Harry, if I take my leave of you. I doubt I would be very pleasant company tonight. I shall see you tomorrow."

"Pleasant company is vastly overrated. Stay awhile. We can drink ourselves under the table and then—"

"Thank you, but I tried that, if you recall, and I've no desire to repeat the experience." He managed a wry smile and added, "Besides, I have to write to my mother, and I shall certainly need a clear head for that."

He left the coffee room without looking around, thankful he was near the door and would not have to endure any more well-wishers. Amazing how quickly gossip spread in London. By morning there would not be a soul in Town who did not know of his impending marriage.

During the short ride in a hackney to his inn, Leo thought of Gillian, trying to devise in his mind a way of setting her down on paper that would appease his mother. It proved a fruitless venture as the spoiled sheets of foolscap crumpled near his desk several hours later indicated. His mother would demand to know who the girl's people were—and what could he say? Her father is a financier so wealthy he could buy most of England and not feel the pinch—but utterly lacking in taste and refinement? He could imagine his mother, standing on her dignity, an invisible line of Thackerys and Reeds stretching beyond her . . . his mother who knew the antecedents of her notable family in England . . . Gillian who?

He crumpled another sheet of paper.

While Leo toiled at his task, Gillian, clad in dressing gown and slippers, stood at the window in her bedchamber. She had retired to bed hours earlier, but her mind was too restless to permit her to sleep. She drew open the window slightly, welcoming the rush of cool night air on her flushed cheeks. Gazing down at the moonlit square, she tried to find a measure of relief from her chaotic thoughts, but her mind kept returning to her impending marriage. She traced the line of her lips with her finger, remembering again the exquisite enjoyment of Lord Wrexham's kisses . . . Leo, she silently amended, then sighed.

He'd told her kisses were a prelude to seduction, which was necessary if she were to give him an heir. Although he had not said so, she knew he meant necessary, as in required, as in part of the bargain, and bestowed without personal regard. It would not do to place too great a value on his lordship's kisses. He had merely been testing her.

Lucy, when questioned, said that most likely Lord Wrexham had kissed a lot of ladies—most gentlemen did. And, she'd added, most men weren't above chasing after maids, either, and trying to do more than steal a kiss. Unfortunately, having been strictly reared at the foundling home, she had as little notion of what came after the kisses as did Gillian.

"All I know, miss, is that it ain't something a respectable girl does. Matron warned us against it. She said never let a man put his hand on your chest or beneath your skirt, cause then you'd lie down with him, and when you got up, you would be with child and turned off without character, and the poor babe would have to be left at the door of the foundling home just like I was. And if I was you, miss, I wouldn't be a-letting his lordship kiss you no more until his ring is on your finger."

Gillian had agreed, although Leo had shown no sign of wishing to repeat the experience once they'd left his home—not even after he and her father had come to an agreement over the marriage settlements. Leo had come to her in the drawing room to tell her so, and Papa, over Mrs. Ledbetter's objections, had left them alone for a quarter hour.

Papa needn't have bothered, Gillian thought, for her betrothed had not uttered a word or made a gesture that could not have been witnessed by all of London. Not that she wished him to behave improperly—naturally she did not. But some slight sign that he held her in a small degree of affection would have been welcomed. When he had kissed her earlier, she'd felt a sudden and quite inexplicable warmth toward him and had hoped that her regard was returned. Apparently, it was not.

Gillian shivered suddenly. She drew the window closed, securely latched it, then scampered across the room to the high four-poster bed. As she climbed in and pulled the covers about her, she thought how foolish it was to trouble herself over something so inconsequential. In a year or so, she would return to Richmond and her beloved Willowglen. Compared to that, his lordship matter not at all. Or very little.

Chapter 6

"So, my dear, what time may we expect Lord Wrexham to call?" Oliver Prescott asked as he fondly observed his daughter across the breakfast table. He knew perfectly well that his lordship was due at half past one, but it provided him with a great deal of pleasure to inquire in front of the four footmen stationed about the room. His little girl receiving the Earl of Wrexham! His wife, God rest her sweet soul, would indeed be pleased.

Gillian, knowing what he was about, despised such pretension—but she also understood his pride was not for himself, but for her, and so answered gently, "This afternoon, Papa. He hopes to be here soon after one o'clock, certainly no later than two. He is closeted with his man of business this morning, and apparently there is much that requires his attention."

"I am not surprised," Mrs. Ledbetter remarked with a superior smile. "When a gentleman like Lord Wrexham chooses to wed, there is far more involved than merely posting the banns and placing an announcement in the paper. Naturally arrangements must be made for his particular friends to meet you, not to mention relatives. La, my dear Gillian, a veritable flood of invitations shall be forthcoming! I doubt we shall dine at home above one night in a month. And once you are wed, my dear, as the new Countess of Wrexham, you will be presented to Her Majesty. Now, do not blush, Gillian. I shall be here to guide you through it all. You may place the utmost dependence on me."

"What happens to the old one?" Oliver asked.

"I beg your pardon?"

"The old Lady Wrexham—his lordship's mama. Stands to reason there can't be two Lady Wrexhams wandering about."

Mrs. Ledbetter smiled, a trifle condescendingly. "Oh, indeed not, my dear Mr. Prescott. She—that is, the present Lady Wrexham—will become the Dowager Countess, or she may be referred to by her given name preceding the title, as Anne, Lady Wrexham. Not that I mean to imply that Anne is her ladyship's name, for I am not well acquainted with her, but we shall learn all these details when she comes to Town."

"Seems hard on the old girl to me," Oliver replied as he motioned for a footman to remove his plate. "Gillian, I shouldn't be at all surprised if she takes you into dislike because of it. You shall have to make a push to win her over. Perhaps we should send her a present. Ask his lordship what she might like. Something grand—tell him I'm well able to stand the nonsense."

"Yes, Papa," his daughter replied dutifully, but she had the feeling that her future mother-in-law would dislike her for more reasons than usurping the title, and a gift, no matter how grand, was unlikely to assuage her feelings. Leo had said little about his mother, but Gillian gathered the lady was of uncertain health and uneven temperament. She would not relinquish her position as mistress of Farthingale easily, and certainly not to someone whom she would undoubtedly consider unsuitable.

However, Gillian had no wish to distress her father and she hid her uneasiness behind a sunny smile. As he came around the table, she dutifully lifted her head for his kiss.

"I shall leave such discussions to you ladies. I have

78

business in the city, puss, so you give his lordship my regards."

"Yes, Papa, but I do wish you would reconsider and join us this evening."

"I told you, my girl, I'll not be hanging on his lordship's coattails. Fine thing it would be to have me tagging along, likely as not, embarrassing the pair of you. Now, I wish to hear no more on that score."

When Oliver had quit the room, Mrs. Ledbetter reached over and patted Gillian's hand. "My dear, I cannot think it wise of you to press your papa to push himself forward. He is not accustomed to moving in the first circles of Society, and to insist he join you in such amusements as the theater would mean placing him in a position where he might well be an object of ridicule—and I know you cannot wish that."

Her temper rising, Gillian drawled softly, "There is no one more kind or generous or good than my father. I may frequently be at points with him, but I am not ashamed of him."

"You quite misunderstand me, my dear. I mean not the least disrespect to your father but seek only to spare him the discomfort that must arise when one finds oneself in such elevated company as Lord Wrexham."

With a smile that did not quite reach her eyes, Gillian rose. "I must acquit you then of ingratitude for scorning one who provides for you so generously. My apologies, Mrs. Ledbetter. I should have realized that you were speaking with the true voice of experience. Pray, do excuse me."

Gillian swept out of the room with an air of dignity that would have done justice to a royal princess—but inside she seethed. She loathed London. She loathed the people, particularly those like Mrs. Ledbetter who seemed to think no one of any value or account unless they had been born into the ranks of the aristocracy.

Gillian sighed. Neither she nor Papa belonged in England, and she only wished he could be brought to realize it. But he was as bad as Mrs. Ledbetter. He truly believed he was unworthy to associate with the members of the peerage, and nothing she could say would change his mind.

She spent an unprofitable morning, changing her walking dress several times and having Lucy recomb her hair in a variety of styles, none of which proved the least flattering. At last, she chose a blue silk with a frilled bodice, tiny puffed sleeves laced with ribbons, and a matching ribbon that ran beneath her breast and tied in a bow. Gillian did not particularly like the dress, but she knew it to be the most fashionable she owned. Resigned, she covered her crimped curls with a stylish bonnet adorned with several ostrich feathers dyed to match her gown. The wide-brimmed hat did not become her, either, but had the advantage of hiding most of her hair.

"Are you sure, miss? I thought the green—" Lucy began.

"I am not changing my dress yet again," Gillian interrupted. "Lord Wrexham knows I am neither a beauty nor stylishly fashionable. Indeed, I am certain my appearance cannot be of the least interest to him."

Lucy bit her lip. Her young lady was rarely out of temper, but when she was, it did not pay to argue with her. Miss Gillian could be as difficult as her papa when she was blue-deviled—and Lucy could see something had occurred to dreadfully overset her. The maid watched her mistress pull on her gloves with such force, it was a wonder the seams did not split.

"I am going down to the garden, Lucy. Please let me know when his lordship arrives."

Gillian stepped into the hall, hesitated, then turned to the right and slipped down the rear stairs, which were generally used by only the servants. She nodded to the parlor maid and one of the footmen, but managed to safely escape into the small garden without encountering her companion. She simply could not bear to listen to any more of Mrs. Ledbetter's strictures today.

Once outside, Gillian discovered the sun had burned off the morning fog and the afternoon promised to be delightfully warm—fortunately so, since she'd left her shawl in her room. She paced for several moments, relieving the frustration she'd felt, and, as usual, the exercise combined with the serenity of the garden did much to restore her composure.

Feeling calmer, she seated herself on one of the stone benches and contemplated the afternoon before her. Leo had said he wished to introduce her to a dear friend of his, Lady Tyndale. He described her as elderly and explained that because of rheumatism in her legs, she rarely left her house. Nevertheless, Lady Tyndale was acquainted with most everyone in Town who mattered, and could always be relied upon to know the latest *on dits*. Leo said she would be furious with him should he not bring Gillian to call.

And just what did one say to such a paragon? Gillian stood and curtsied to the rosebush spreading its prickly branches next to the bench. "I am pleased to meet you, Lady Tyndale. Lord Wrexham speaks very highly of you."

Gillian wrinkled her nose at the bush. Witty repartee it was not. She curtsied again and drawled, "I am charmed to meet you, my lady. Dear Wrexham quite insisted we call—oh, fiddle-faddle. If I spoke the truth, Madam Bush, I would tell you that I most sincerely wish you and all the others of your kind would fall into the River Thames—"

"I hope that does not include the gentlemen of your acquaintance."

Gillian whirled about at the sound of the deep male voice, and blushed a fiery red. "Lord Wrexham!"

"Did I startle you, my dear?" he asked apologetically as he joined her beside the bench. "I do apologize, but when your butler said you were in the garden, I claimed the privilege of seeking you out myself."

Avoiding his eyes, she gestured toward the bush. "You must consider me a perfect imbecile, my lord. I was only trying to think of what to say to someone like Lady Tyndale. I have not had much experience with the nobility."

He took her hand in his and drew her down to sit beside him on the bench. "What I think is that you are very sweet, and just a bit nervous at meeting Lady Tyndale—though you need not be. She is Harry's aunt, you know, and a trifle eccentric. Truth to tell, I believe she would have been much amused had she heard you just now."

"If you mean she would have laughed at me—"

"No, Gillian, not at all. Lady Tyndale has scant patience with most of the ladies of her acquaintance and has frequently wished worse on them than a dip in the Thames."

"Truly, my lord?" she asked, head still bowed.

"Truly. Now, pray tell me what I have done to displease you. Yesterday you called me Leo. Has my esteem with you dropped so low that you feel compelled to address me formally?"

She ducked her head. "I fear I am not yet accustomed to addressing you in such a manner."

"Are you quite certain that is all, my dear? I will understand if, having been granted time to reconsider, you have changed your mind. Gillian, look at me. I would have the truth."

She lifted her head, gazing shyly into his gray eyes. "I have no wish to alter our arrangements . . . Leo."

"I am relieved to hear you say so, for I have begun to

think that we will deal exceptionally well together. And now, my dear, unless you wish to offend Lady Tyndale by a tardy arrival, we must leave." He rose as he spoke and drew her to her feet, then smiled teasingly. "Of course, 'tis quite private here—we might tarry awhile longer. I have no objection."

He leaned down, brushing her lips lightly with his own. It was not a passionate kiss, but a gentle caress that did much to restore her confidence. When he lifted his head, her blue eyes glimmered with suppressed laughter. She tucked her hand in his arm and mockingly rebuked, "Leo! Alas, I see I shall have to be one of those nagging wives forever scolding her husband to see he keeps his appointments in a timely manner."

"If this is your notion of scolding, I foresee I shall be the most contented of husbands."

Despite assurances from her betrothed, Gillian was astonished by Lady Tyndale—and her home. Neither was what she expected. Leo had not thought to mention that the elderly woman who commanded London Society stood five feet nothing in her stockings, weighed less than seven stone, or that her affliction had left her face ravaged by pain and her hands nearly as crippled as her legs. She received her guests seated in a high-backed chair placed at the far end of an immense drawing room, her small, brilliant eyes watching as they approached.

The rest of her body might be wasted, but those eyes were as alive and burning as the coals glowing in the fireplace to the lady's right. At first Gillian had been intimidated, but after a moment of intense scrutiny, Lady Tyndale looked up at Leo and laughed. "She'll do, Wrexham, though you surprise me. I had not thought you had so much good sense."

Unoffended, he bowed over her hand and replied gallantly, "It must always be an object with me to please you."

"Then it's a pity you never made more of an effort—you and Harry. Rapscallions, the pair of you. He's here somewhere—go find him and leave me to talk to this child for a few moments." Gillian was bidden to be seated in a chair drawn near the fire.

She did so, sitting on the edge, her back rigidly straight, her hands folded in her lap, and her chin held high. She knew how much regard Leo held for Lady Tyndale, and she was prepared to be courteous, but she couldn't help wishing he had not left her alone. Her eyes followed him as he made his way through the room, greeting various ladies and gentlemen, then disappearing through the double doors set open at the far end.

"You will do well, Miss Prescott, to set a guard on your emotions."

Startled, Gillian turned her attention to Lady Tyndale. "I beg your pardon?"

"Disabuse your mind of the notion that you are among friends in this room. With the exception of myself, Wrexham, and possibly my nephew, I doubt there are any present who wish you well. You have three marks against you, my dear."

Gillian smiled ruefully. "Only three?"

Lady Tyndale leaned forward, her thin shoulders hunched as she rested her weight against the ebony cane clutched in her hands. "Wrexham is dear to me, and I would not see him unhappy. Therefore, I am prepared to help you. Now then, do you know what these people hold against you?"

Almost against her will, Gillian felt compelled to answer. In a low voice she said, "Birth, breeding, and . . . I suppose, my appearance."

"Bah, your looks have nothing to do with the matter. If they did, half the ton would be outcasts. As for your birth, 'tis unremarkable. True, your father is not what one would wish, but your mother was a Davenport. You have nothing to blush for there."

"I assure you, I do not, Lady Tyndale, nor for my father, and I should also tell you, my lady, that I do not aspire to figure in the ranks of the ton."

"Your sentiments do you credit, my dear, but we are discussing Wrexham. If you wish to be a credit to him, then you will heed what I have to say and cease quibbling with me. There are those in this room who resent you because you are an American—" She broke off to raise her cane, using it to wave away a gentleman who had started to approach her. "Mushroom," she muttered, then turned to Gillian again. "What was I saying?"

"That people will resent me because I am an American."

"Not only an American, but a wealthy one. There are those who will always envy great riches, my dear. And what is worse, you have had the audacity to snare a very personable young lord who, had not the Fates intervened, was destined to wed one of their own. I presume you know about Miss Beauclerk?"

Blushing, Gillian nodded. "I am sincerely sorry for her."

"Don't be. Miss Beauclerk will have no trouble acquiring another beau, one who, hopefully, will be better suited to her than Wrexham. A more ill-conceived match I cannot imagine, though both of them were too infatuated to see the truth of the matter. You are what he needs, Miss Prescott."

Gillian blushed anew. She could not tell Lady Tyndale that her impending marriage was merely a convenience to enable her to return to America as soon as possible.

"You must stop blushing, child. It gives away your feelings too plainly."

"I am sorry, my lady, but I cannot seem to help it," Gillian answered, turning a brighter red.

"Well, perhaps we may turn it to your advantage. Now—blast, I cannot talk to you here," she muttered as another couple approached and stood waiting at a discreet distance. "Tell Wrexham you are to dine with me on Thursday. I shall expect you at six."

Realizing she was dismissed, Gillian rose and curtsied politely. The room yawned before her, and she was aware of a dozen interested gazes turned in her direction. She kept her eyes focused on the double doors at the end of the room, wishing Leo would appear. No one made the smallest effort to smile at her, or nod or bow. Even a prisoner approaching the gallows received more encouragement, Gillian thought, as she slowly walked through the room. She heard the hum of conversation rise and fall as she passed, and knew she was the object of much discussion. Well, let them talk. She lifted her chin another inch, regretted again that she was not taller and of more regal bearing, and at last reached the entrance to the second salon.

She immediately perceived the difference between the rooms. In the salon dominated by Lady Tyndale's high-backed chair, the guests had either strolled about or stood in small clusters, talking quietly. The effect was of a refined, dignified gathering. But in here the air vibrated with the sound of animated conversation and bursts of frequent laughter. Many of the ladies and gentlemen were seated on the various sofas, settees, and chairs, which had been arranged in small groupings for ease in conversing. Liveried footmen, splendid in their cream uniforms embroidered with deep blue and gold facings, passed among the guests, offering glasses of champagne or an assortment of delicate cakes and cookies from their silver trays.

However, one commonality marked the rooms. No one paid the least attention to Gillian as she paused at the entrance. Her anxious eyes searched for Leo, but his tall, black-clad figure was not in evidence. He must be in the last of the three rooms thrown open for Lady Tyndale's guests, she thought, and hesitated. Her nature was not cowardly, but to walk the length of yet another room unattended was slightly more than she could bear.

Just beyond the door, Gillian spotted a secluded alcove that was shielded from prying eyes by an ornate Chinese screen and several large, potted shrubs. Aware of several covert glances in her direction, she assumed an air of purpose and walked directly to the alcove, where she sank with relief onto a delicately carved, beautifully covered love seat. A casement window above her provided a fine view of the road, and for several minutes she amused herself by watching a variety of carriages arrive and depart. But the diversion paled quickly, and she wondered how long it would be before Leo came in search of her.

Although the screen effectively blocked her view of the room, she could hear snippets of conversation and listened intently for the sound of one particular deep voice.

She heard several young ladies discussing a new shop on Ludgate Hill, where tremendous bargains might be obtained, and an older woman enumerating her ailments, of which there were so many, Gillian wondered the woman could walk at all. Apparently she could, for the sound of her conversation drifted away. Then a pair of male voices floated over the screen. Gillian eavesdropped as they debated the merits of a newly purchased mare, but neither voice belonged to Leo. She was about to go in search of him, when she heard his name mentioned.

"Wrexham's always had the devil's own luck."

"Don't be taken in—if you ask me, he's putting on a brave front. Halbert told me Wrexham had to be helped from the Guards' Club the other night, he was so drunk.

And have you seen his heiress? I hear she's a timid little thing with neither style nor conversation."

"Ah, well, it hardly matters, does it? 'Tis not beauty Wrexham seeks, but a fortune. Pity though about Miss Beauclerk. Think she'll have Fenwick now?"

"They're betting four to one at White's . . ."

As the gentlemen's voices faded, Gillian stared blindly out the window. She remembered a governess at Willowglen once telling her that eavesdroppers never heard good of themselves, and blinked back foolish tears.

"Miss Prescott?"

Gillian glanced around and saw Sir Harry approaching. She sniffed, achieved a credible smile, and held out her hand.

"I have been searching everywhere for you. Leo sent me to rescue you from my aunt," he said as he bowed. Then he looked more closely and saw the sparkle of tears still wet on her lashes. "My dear, did she say something to offend you? You must not mind. Indeed, 'tis something of a distinction to receive one of my aunt's scolds. You will not credit it, but she once told the Prince Regent that he needed to diet. He has been wearing corsets ever since—not that it answers, for they squeak whenever he moves. Most embarrassing, I assure you. Of course, everyone pretends not to notice, but I pray he does not call here. I fear Aunt Seraphina would not hesitate to bring it to his attention."

"Perhaps Lady Tyndale did not like me, then," Gillian replied. "She was exceedingly kind and invited me to dine on Thursday."

His brows rose and mischief danced in his blue eyes. "Miss Prescott, you have been singularly honored. Does Leo know—is he bidden to escort you?"

"She said I was to tell him, but I have not seen him . . ."

"He is in the next room, held captive by half a dozen military-mad young scamps who would know every detail of his last campaign. One would think it was Wellington himself come home, the way they question him. I expect he awaits only your appearance to make his escape. Shall we rescue him?"

Gillian looked down at her gloved hands and spoke so softly, he had to lean forward to catch her words. "Would you be so kind as to bring Lord Wrexham to me? I should like to sit here yet awhile."

"Then, I shall join you," Harry replied, and without waiting for permission sat down beside her. "Now, Miss Prescott, if not my aunt, who has been unkind to you? The truth now, for I am Leo's best friend, and I won't be fobbed off with a Banbury tale."

"No one," she stammered, but her blushes betrayed her. Aware of Sir Harry's intent gaze, she added, "Truly, sir, no one has spoken a word to me since I left your aunt. She did warn me that I should be resented because of . . . Miss Beauclerk."

"Did she, now?" Harry asked, drumming his fingers against the knee of his buff pantaloons. "I suppose some people might hold that against you, but there are others, Miss Prescott, like myself, who believe Leo is better off than he knows. He will come to realize it himself, given time."

Much heartened, Gillian found the courage to ask, "Is she very beautiful?"

"Miss Beauclerk? I suppose so, in a sort of boring, predictable way. She is blond, with pretty green eyes and a pale countenance and most sensitive—"

Beginning to enjoy herself, Gillian interrupted, "You find that a fault, sir? I confess I am most sensitive myself, and . . . and given to blushing."

"You, my dear, blush in a very modest way. Miss Beauclerk goes you one better and faints whenever her sensibilities are overcome, which is quite often. I believe that makes some gentlemen feel protective of her."

She laughed. "But not you?"

"No, I fear I have scant patience with such dramatics. My taste tends toward petite ladies with a great deal of character, particularly those with red hair and entrancing blue eyes."

Gillian blushed and turned away from his teasing eyes. "I protest, sir. You are making sport of me."

"Not at all," he replied, capturing one of her gloved hands. "I am merely endeavoring to point out that you need not stand in Miss Beauclerk's shadow."

She shook her head despairingly. "I fear there can be no comparison. I have heard it said that I possess neither style nor wit, and I need no one to tell me that I shall never be a beauty."

"Nonsense!" he retorted. He looked at her, assessing both her faults and her virtues, hesitated, then plunged ahead. "Miss Prescott, may I be frank with you? I do not wish to offend you, but your dress, your hat, the manner in which you wear your hair, ill becomes you. My dear, you need someone to take you in hand."

She fingered the folds of her new walking dress. "I confess I do not quite like it, but I was assured this style was the latest mode."

"It is indeed, and you may trust my judgment in such matters, but it does not suit you. You are too tiny, too delicate to wear such lacy frills and ribbons. Your hats, too, should be small so that they permit one to see the exquisite shape of your face. And your hair—my dear, I beg you, do not allow anyone to insist on so many curls."

"But it is the style," she protested.

"You shall set your own style, and I shall help you— that is, if you are willing?"

She looked up at him and answered honestly, "I should be glad of your assistance, sir, but ... why do you trouble yourself? We have met but briefly, so I do not flatter myself that you care what becomes of me."

"I am rapidly beginning to, Miss Prescott," he said, smiling down at her. "But, in truth, 'tis for Leo's sake. He is like a brother to me—"

"And you do not wish him to be embarrassed," Gillian finished. "Very well, then. What must I do?"

It was not what he'd intended to say, but he saw no reason to tell her that Leo had been in love with Diana Beauclerk for several years—or at least fancied himself in love. Harry had dreaded their marriage, fearing it would drive a wedge between them, for he had no high opinion of the lady, and she knew it. He had feared, too, that once the dew was off the rose, Leo would discover his lady was all show and no substance. But now, all that was changed, and he grinned down at Miss Prescott. "Be ready at eleven in the morning. I shall call for you then."

"Eleven! So early, sir?"

"We have much to do, my dear. Now, come. We had best find Leo or he will think I am trying to cut him out."

She laughed at such an absurd notion, and such was her amusement with Harry that she passed through the salons without noticing the ladies who stared at her and whispered behind their fans.

Chapter 7

Wrexham handed his hat and gloves to the butler, inquiring softly, "How is she, Piedmore?"

"As well as may be expected, my lord. She is resting in the rose drawing room. Lady Clarissa is sitting with her."

Leo nodded, and mounted the stairs. It was little more than he'd anticipated. He could only be thankful that his elder sister, Jane, due to an outbreak of measles in her own household, had been unable to accompany their mother to Town. Jane had not only inherited Lady Wrexham's frail health, but also a tendency to prophesy doom at the least setback, and, since her marriage, a lamentable habit of quoting her husband on every occasion. Leo did not doubt that "dear Cecil" had very decided opinions of his brother-in-law's betrothal, and Jane would not hesitate to share them.

Naturally, he held for his elder sister the regard and esteem due her—but he was not overly fond of Jane, perhaps due to the disparity in their ages. Like John, she was several years older. She had been presented to Society when Leo was twelve, and had frequently complained of him and Harry. Grubby schoolboys was one of her kinder epithets, Leo remembered with a grin.

As for Clarissa, he was not well acquainted with her, either, but he could not imagine she would be of much assistance. Just sixteen, she was not yet out, and he had seen little of her when he had come home for the funerals. He rather thought she took after their father, and would be a pretty girl when her eyes were not red-rimmed from tears.

Bracing himself for the worst, he opened the door of the drawing room.

Lavinia, gold curls peeping out from beneath a most becoming lace cap, reclined on the rose sofa. Resplendent in a black gown with white lace at her sleeves and throat, she appeared elegantly pale. Hearing a footstep, she lifted her head from the pillows plumped behind her on the sofa and looked around. Perceiving her son, she cried out faintly, "Leopold—at last you have come! My son, oh, my dearest son, I thought never to see you again."

Clarissa stood behind her mother. Attired in a sprigged muslin gown, with her dark curls tied back with a blue ribbon, she presented a pleasing appearance. Grinning at her brother, she explained, "When you were not here to greet us, Mama quite thought a disaster must have befallen you."

"But didn't Piedmore explain that I had business to attend to this afternoon? I am quite sure I left word that I would return after paying calls, and I've just finished now."

Lavinia, her smelling salts in one hand, a dainty vinaigrette clutched in the other, moaned softly. With her eyes closed, she murmured, "I suppose it is too much to expect you to enter into my emotions, but when a woman has lost her husband and her eldest son . . . alas, if only John were here. He would know how dreadfully my heart is breaking."

"But, Mama, if John were here, then you would not be grieving for him," Clarissa pointed out.

Lavinia opened her eyes and glared at her youngest. "You are an unfeeling girl, and I cannot think how I came to have such unnatural children! Is it not sufficient that I shall never again feel sweet little Millicent's arms about my neck, that my dearest John was most cruelly wrenched from me, that Jane has deserted me in my hour of need, and Leopold—on whom I had placed all my dependence—Leopold does not deem it of sufficient importance to be on hand to greet his mother? I declare, I do not know what I have done to be treated so shabbily."

"Now, Mama, I am quite certain that between Piedmore and Siddons, you have been well taken care of," Leo said as he crossed the room and drew up a chair next to the sofa.

"Servants are not the same as family," Lady Wrexham replied depressingly. "And I might remind you, Leopold, that I journeyed to Town at great expense and discomfort to myself because you expressly wished for my attendance. Though had I but known to what indignities I should be subjected—the inn where we were forced to put up was shockingly vulgar, and I daresay had not Siddons thought to bring our own sheets, I could not have borne to sleep in the bed."

Surprised, Leo said, "The White Hart? I own I am astonished."

"We did not stop there," Clarissa informed him, her lively eyes dancing. "The White Hart was full due to a prizefight in town, and dozens of gentlemen and military men had claimed all the rooms. One of them did offer us his—"

"Impertinent jackanapes," her mother interrupted. "Naturally, we could not stay there, and no other accommodations were to be had for miles. A disgusting sport, boxing, and I cannot think why gentlemen are so mad for it."

"Well, I am sorry you should have been so troubled, but you are here now, Mama, and you have your own comfortable room—"

"My room?" she reproached, her voice rising. "For how long, may I ask, before that . . . that person you plan

94

to marry in such shocking haste claims it for her own? And Farthingale, too!" She moaned, and leaned her head back against the cushions. "I doubt I can bear it, to see another set in my place, to see another in the house that holds so many dear memories, so much history—"

"And so many drafty corners and smoking chimneys," Clarissa interrupted. "Come, Mama, you are forever complaining how inconvenient it is. Why, before Papa died, you said it was your dearest wish to remove to that sweet little house in Bath."

Lavinia had resorted to her smelling salts, and Leo frowned at his sister.

"Well, it's true," she said. "You have not been much at home, Leo, but Farthingale is in need of great repair. Even Papa said that when he came about again, he would have to lay aside some blunt to set it right."

"Clarissa, I will thank you not to use cant expressions. As for Farthingale, you are too young to understand the sentiment attached to one's ancestral home. 'Tis true I may have complained on occasion, but that does not lessen my feeling on seeing it pass to one who cannot possibly understand its history, or its worth. And in such unseemly haste. Leopold, if, as you have written, it is necessary to marry this . . . this American, must you do so at once? It is indecent to be thinking of nuptials when we are still in deep mourning for your dear father and brother."

"I am aware of how trying it must be for you, Mama, but if I am to save Farthingale, I must wed at once. Mr. Prescott will brook no delay—nor will my creditors."

"He sounds most disagreeable," Lavinia complained, and lifted her vinaigrette as though even pronouncing his name produced an offensive odor.

"His manners are somewhat rough," Leo conceded, "but he has been extremely generous, and you must realize how deeply we shall be indebted to him. I hope when he and Miss Prescott come here this evening, you will—"

"I cannot possibly see them," she interrupted. "You cannot ask it of me, Leopold, not today. Have you no feelings? Do you not comprehend the trials I have endured? My head is throbbing, and I feel dreadfully faint. You shall have to make my excuses."

He stared at her for a moment, then sighed. "Clarissa, would you leave us, please?"

"Why? I am not a child any longer, Leo, and the future of Farthingale concerns me as much as it does Mama. Besides, if she faints, you will have need of me."

"In that event, I shall be certain to send for you," he replied as he rose to his feet. He came around the sofa, took her firmly by the shoulders, and turned her toward the door. "Please oblige me, Clarissa. I wish to speak to Mama privately."

"Oh, very well, but 'tis monstrous unfair. No one ever tells me anything."

Leo smiled at her, watched for a moment as she walked down the hall to make certain she did not linger outside the door, then closed it firmly.

Lavinia, from her place on the sofa, glanced at him with something like fear in her eyes. "Good gracious, Leopold, for a moment you put me quite in mind of your father."

He did not reply but came to stand by the sofa, looking gravely down at her. "If you do not want me to wed Miss Prescott, pray say so at once. I do not wish to do anything which would ill affect your health—"

"That is very good of you, Leopold. I knew that you would have a care—"

"However," he continued, his voice rising over hers, "if that is your decision, you should be aware that not only will Farthingale be sold, but this house as well, and the farms in York. You and Clarissa will have the house in Bath and a small—a very small—jointure. Our debts will be such that you will not be able to order so much as a pair of gloves on credit. Of course, you could live with Jane, but I—"

"Stop!" his mother cried, covering her ears. "Oh, if only your father or John were alive to hear you speak to me so!"

"If either were alive, this conversation would not be necessary." He sat down in the chair drawn near the sofa. "Unfortunately, they are not, and we are left in regrettably straitened circumstances. The choice is yours, Mama. We can accept Mr. Prescott's exceedingly generous offer, or we can live like paupers."

"Hardly a choice, Leopold." She sniffed. "And you know I could never live with Jane."

He smiled at that. "I know, and I regret this is all so disagreeable for you. A marriage of convenience is not what I would choose either, but once having agreed, you must see that we are greatly in Prescott's debt. I will not have him meet with ingratitude or disrespect in this house."

"Heavens, Leopold, I only said that I was not well enough to come down for dinner. Surely he would understand," she began, but as she saw the look in his eyes, hastily amended, "Very well. Though it pains me, I shall receive this man. Now, go away, and send Siddons to me."

Leo, sitting at the head of the table that evening, thought his dinner party the most uncomfortable he'd ever attended. His mother, at the opposite end of the table, bore the regal air of a queen who had condescended to dine with the commoners. Although she was not precisely rude, she spoke with such icy reserve that neither Mr. Prescott, seated to her right, nor Harry, on her left, was able to draw her into a prolonged conversation—though Harry, bless him, tried.

If Lady Wrexham intended by her manner to put Oliver Prescott firmly in his place, she failed miserably. Noticing that she had not partaken of much to eat, Oliver suggested she try the ham, which was delightfully done to a turn. When her ladyship declined, remarking in throbbing tones that she had not much of an appetite, he recommended a dish of apples and dried plums.

"Probably a touch of irregularity," he told her. "I get it myself whenever I travel. These youngsters here, they don't know what it is to have a sensitive stomach, eh, your ladyship? But plums and apples will set you straight. You try it and see if I'm not right."

Clarissa, seated between Oliver and her brother, heard him and, betwixt a gurgle of laughter and swallowing a sip of lemonade, nearly choked. He turned his attention immediately to her, clapped her heartily on the back, and recommended she take a deep breath.

"Went down the wrong way, did it?" He chuckled. "Now, if that had been a chicken bone, you might have been in trouble. Saw a man choke to death once that way. Terrible thing, terrible."

"Did he die?" she asked, her gray eyes round with curiosity. She had never encountered anyone like Mr. Prescott. Although she'd been prepared to quite dislike him, she found him full of good humor, attentive to her, and ready to indulge her as her own father had never done.

"Clarissa," her brother reproved. "I hardly think that a suitable topic for the dinner table."

"Your brother's right, my dear, but it's me he should be chawing down, not you. You're a pretty behaved girl, and it 'pears to me you've had a rough time of it. Now then, what can I do to see that you have a bit of fun while you're in Town? Do you fancy the theater, or perhaps the circus?"

On the opposite side of the table, seated between Sir Harry and Lord Wrexham, Gillian prayed that the interminable meal would come to an end. Her father was trying so hard to please, but it seemed to her that every time he opened his mouth, he said precisely the wrong thing. And now Papa was making plans to take Lady Clarissa out, and Gillian could tell from Leo's frown that he did not approve of the scheme. Would the meal never end?

She laid down her fork. Although she was certain the food was delicious, Gillian was far too nervous to eat more than a few bites. She took another sip of wine, then very carefully placed her glass on the table. Almost instantly, a footman was at her side to refill it. Leo's servants were exceedingly well trained, she observed, and wondered if Lady Wrexham was responsible. Of course she was. Gillian remembered Leo saying that he owned several properties in addition to Farthingale. And soon she herself would be in charge of those households. Daunted, she took another sip of wine.

"My dear, you have barely touched your food. May I offer you some fresh peaches, or strawberries?" Leo asked, concern showing in his eyes.

"Nothing, thank you," she murmured. "I fear I have not much of an appetite this evening. I suppose 'tis the . . . the excitement of meeting your family. Your sister is a lovely girl."

He spared a glance for Clarissa, who was chuckling aloud at something Prescott had said. Her irrepressible sense of humor had obviously found a kindred spirit. Leo only hoped it would not lead her to behave in an unbecoming manner. He had already noticed his mother eyeing her several times, and feared his sister was in for a scold—but Clarissa could take care of herself.

To Gillian, he said, "She is enjoying the evening immensely, thanks to your father. 'Tis very kind of him to pay her so much attention."

"But you wish he would not," Gillian replied softly, then blushed furiously. She had not meant to say the words aloud, but the wine had loosened her tongue. Perhaps it was just as well, for she saw the truth on his stricken face. "I will warn him off, my lord."

Before Leo could respond, his mother rose, signaling it was time for the ladies to withdraw. He came around the table to assist Gillian, but she would have none of his help, and left the room with her back held as rigidly straight as his mother's.

Oliver Prescott clapped him on the shoulder. "Well, my lord, 'tis my opinion that dinner went off rather well. I don't say your mother don't cut up a trifle stiff, but that's only to be expected, and she'll come around, I don't doubt. As for your sister, she's a taking little puss. I only wish my Gillian had some of her vivacity."

Sir Harry was the first to take his leave. It was early, not quite ten, but Leo did not press him to remain. Harry was a staunch friend—he had not only attended what was undeniably the most tedious dinner party in history—but also made the best of a lamentable evening. Leo saw him out, regretfully declined an invitation to join him at the Guards' Club, and returned to his guests.

As if Harry's leave-taking was their cue, everyone began to make farewells. Leo put a restraining hand on Prescott's arm and said, "I have a boon to ask of you, sir."

"Name it, my lord, and 'tis yours."

Leo laughed. "You are very generous, Mr. Prescott, but I shall not take much advantage of you. 'Tis only that I should like permission to drive Gillian home myself."

"Leopold!" his mother protested. "Surely you are not

planning to go out? Why, I have scarce had a word with you, and there is much we need to discuss."

"But, Mama, you just said you could not wait to seek the comfort of your bed," Clarissa pointed out.

Blushing, Gillian drew her shawl closer about her shoulders. "Perhaps, my lord, tomorrow would be—"

"Nonsense, puss," her father interrupted, and winked broadly at Lady Wrexham. "Her ladyship and I ain't so old we've forgotten what 'tis like to be newly betrothed. 'Tis natural his lordship wishes a few moments alone with you. I shall walk down with you." He made an awkward bow to the ladies, then offered his daughter his arm.

Feeling she had little choice, Gillian dropped a curtsy. As she took her leave of Lady Wrexham and Lady Clarissa, she uttered some inanity, but would have been hard-pressed to recall what she said. A moment later, standing on the steps beside Lord Wrexham, she saw her father off, and responded somehow to his teasing that he would send the Bow Street Runners out if she was not home within the hour. Then Leo's coachman appeared in the square with the landau.

She was helped solicitously inside, settled comfortably against the squabs, and heard Leo order his coachman to take the long way around. Gillian was devoutly thankful that the outside carriage lamps provided only the faintest illumination, for she was deeply mortified and knew not where to look or what to say. The evening had been a catastrophe. Leo's mother despised her, and despised Papa. Gillian suspected Lady Wrexham would do her utmost to persuade Leo that the marriage should not go forth—and she could not blame the lady.

Tonight had shown Gillian how far apart their worlds were. Leo was far too well-bred to show his dismay, but she had sensed how embarrassed he was, and how much he disapproved of her father's interest in Lady Clarissa— dear Papa, who had meant only to be kind—would not be considered a suitable person for the Earl of Wrexham's sister to know. Gillian was not surprised Leo desired a word alone with her. He probably could not wait until the morrow to tell her he wished to end their betrothal.

"Gillian, my dear, I owe you an apology," he said, his voice wrapping around her like velvet in the darkness.

"No, my lord, pray do not say so. I . . . I quite understand your dilemma."

"Then you are a saint, but I promise you that once we are wed, you will not be subjected to such tedious evenings. Mama will remove to Bath directly after our wedding, and I doubt she will visit but infrequently. She has never been too fond of Farthingale."

She twisted her gloved hands together. "Is . . . is that what you wished to say to me?"

"Partly," he replied. "I also wanted to discuss your father's attention to Clarissa."

"I know you cannot like it, and I shall—"

"You misunderstand me, Gillian. 'Tis not Clarissa but your father I am concerned about. She is an impudent little minx. I could have strangled her when she had the audacity to provide your father with a list of places she wished to visit, quite as though he had nothing to do but provide for her pleasure."

"But . . . you mean you do not object if Papa wishes to take her to see the Tower of London?"

"Object? On the contrary, I shall be eternally grateful to him for keeping her occupied! Left to her own devices, there is no telling what mischief she would brew, but I cannot allow her to take advantage of his generosity."

"Papa likes her, Leo, and will delight in squiring her about. Oh, yes, truly he will. He tried to persuade me, when we first arrived in Town, to accompany him to all those places the guidebooks say one should see, only 'tis not what I like. But Lady Clarissa—if you are certain you do not mind her being in his company—would enjoy it immensely, I think."

He reached for her hand in the darkness. "I feared you had formed the wrong impression at dinner. My dear, I would be the most ungrateful and ill-mannered boor in history were I to take exception to such kindness."

She sighed and relaxed a little, finding comfort in the closeness of his broad shoulders, then shyly confessed, "When you asked to drive me home, I thought you meant to withdraw from our betrothal."

"So you think me a cad as well as ill-mannered?" he teased. He released her hand and lifted his arm so it circled her shoulders.

She nestled against him, finding it a very pleasant sensation. "You know I do not, and I don't believe anyone even slightly acquainted with you could ever think so."

"Thank you, but you may be assured the world would not share your opinion were I to jilt you. Only a lady may withdraw from an engagement once it is announced. However, I believe that is one problem we need not concern ourselves with unless . . . I hope you do not wish to cry off?"

Gillian, discovering that she was suddenly feeling ridiculously happy and contented, laughed softly. "No, indeed, but I fear your mother is not pleased."

He dropped a featherlight kiss on her brow. "Shall I tell you a secret? It will probably spoil your good opinion of me, for a son should never speak disrespectfully of his parents, but since she will soon be your mother-in-law, I believe there is something you should know."

Startled, she tried to see his eyes, but his face was in shadows and she could not tell if he was serious or merely jesting.

"Mama," he said solemnly, "has little regard for anyone other than herself. When my father was alive, she abused him roundly, which, now that I come to think of it, may be why he spent so little time at home. My elder sister, Jane, according to Mama, is utterly lacking in ambition, dull-witted, and an indifferent mother. My brother, John, when he was alive was deemed a scapegrace and spendthrift without care or consideration for anyone save himself. Of course, now that he has died, he will probably join the rank of Millicent, who, I must warn you, is a positive paragon."

"Millicent? I do not believe I have heard you mention her."

"Possibly not. She was born between John and Jane, and died of smallpox when she was ten. I don't remember her, so perhaps she was saintly, but Jane says she was a nosy little tattler who curried favor with Mama by ratting on the rest of us."

"You have a large family," Gillian replied, a shade wistfully. "I cannot imagine what it would be like living amongst so many brothers and sisters."

"Ask Clarissa," he advised. "I suspect she envies you being an only child and having all your father's attention, not to mention that he seems ready to give you the moon should you suddenly desire it. I heard him telling my sister that he wanted to purchase you a monkey because he heard the Duchess of Avon has one. He seemed much grieved that you did not wish for so fashionable a pet."

"Oh, dear, I hope Lady Clarissa did not express a desire for a monkey?"

"Surely he wouldn't?"

Gillian sighed. "I hope not, for I don't believe your mother would like it, but Papa loves giving presents."

He laughed, his shoulders shaking as he imagined his mother's horror were such an animal delivered to Grosvenor Square. "My dear, do try to restrain him. Tell him it would not be at all appropriate. And speaking of your papa, I believe I had best escort you to the door before he grows impatient. I have seen the curtain at that window pulled aside a dozen times."

Gillian realized abruptly that the carriage had not been moving for some time. She glanced beyond his shoulder and saw they were in Cavendish Square. An impish grin curved her lips. "No doubt Lady Carlisle will be wondering what we are about."

Leo tilted up her chin and kissed her lightly on her lips. Before she could respond, he had withdrawn the arm holding her close, opened the door, and jumped lightly down. He gave her his arm as she came down the steps, and they walked slowly across the square.

"May I call for you tomorrow? I should like to take you to meet my great-aunt. She is elderly and lives quite retired, but I think you would like her."

"To-morrow?" Gillian stammered. "I cannot! I shall be . . . out for most of the day."

"Thursday, then? 'Tis of no great moment. Aunt Augusta is at home every day."

He spoke easily but Gillian had caught the slight note of surprise in his voice that she would be otherwise engaged. She said, "I would change my appointment, but it is with a most highly recommended modiste, and she has set aside this time especially for me."

"Do not give it another thought, then. I shall see you Thursday. Until then, my dear," he said, and bowed gallantly.

Broom had the door open, for he had been on the watch for her. Gillian stepped inside, wishing that she did not have to deceive Leo. But she comforted herself with the knowledge that she had not precisely lied.

Chapter 8

When Leo arrived at the breakfast table the following morning, he found only Clarissa in the dining room to greet him. "Has Mama been down?"

"No, she has one of her megrims and ordered a tray sent up." With blithe unconcern, she added, "Siddons is posted at her door and will admit no one. I expect we shall not see Mama for several days."

Leo, about to take a mouthful of eggs, paused and glanced at his younger sister. "I pray you are jesting."

Surprised, she looked up. "Don't you remember that Mama always takes to her bed whenever she is displeased? Well, perhaps she did not when you were at home, but for years now she has done so. I think she first did so to annoy Papa, but that never answered because he only went away."

"Then she is not ill?"

"Oh, no. 'Tis only she did not like Mr. Prescott, although I think he is the drollest person imaginable. Leo, you will not object if he wishes to take me to Astley's, will you?"

"Clarissa, you must not tease him. Prescott is a financier, and I am sure he has more pressing concerns than taking a schoolroom miss to the circus."

Her gray eyes, so like his own, flashed indignantly. "I did not tease him. He said he could think of nothing he would enjoy more. And I am *not* a schoolroom miss, either. I am turned sixteen, you know."

Leo hid a smile. "I had not realized it, but if so, then I suggest you conduct yourself with more decorum. As for the circus, you must ask Mama's permission."

"She will only say that you are head of the family now, and the decision must be entirely yours. Besides, if he wishes to go today or tomorrow, Siddons will not permit me to see Mama. Please, Leo, say that I may go."

"Let us wait and see if Mr. Prescott broaches the scheme again—"

"But if he does?" she interrupted eagerly.

"I suppose it can do no harm, but, Clarissa, you are not to mention it to him—or the Tower, or the other places you hinted so strongly that you would like to visit."

"I was merely being polite," she replied. "He did ask, you know."

"Perhaps he was merely being polite as well," Leo muttered, and retired behind the pages of the *London Gazette*.

Clarissa subsided. For a few moments she ate heartily of her breakfast while covertly watching her brother. When he lowered his paper to reach for his cup, she said tentatively, "Leo, may I ask you a question?"

With the hope that Gillian was not one of the females who liked to chatter at breakfast, he put down his paper. "If you feel you must."

She hesitated, toyed with her spoon for a moment, then glanced gravely up at him. "Jane said that Cecil thinks you are most admirable."

"Does he, indeed? When next you write Jane, you may tell her that I am vastly indebted to him."

She grinned at that, for she considered her brother-in-law a prosy fellow with too many opinions, but she was not to be diverted. "Leo, are you . . . well, he said that you are making a great sacrifice to save Farthingale, and

Jane said that it must be extremely painful for you to set another in Miss Beauclerk's place."

"I see. And you have been imagining that I am hiding a broken heart behind a cheerful facade, is that it?"

She smiled. "You make it sound so silly, but even Mama said you and Miss Beauclerk were destined for each other. She's so beautiful, I can quite see that you would love her dearly . . . and if that is true, then I think it is horrid that you have to marry Miss Prescott instead."

"Clarissa, you must not—"

"Pray, let me finish. I know you think I am only a foolish schoolgirl, but I am sixteen, Leo, and if anyone must make a sacrifice for the family, I think it should be me. For one thing, I have not yet formed a lasting attachment, and for another, I believe I should quite like being married to a wealthy gentleman."

"Then I hope you may marry one, but not just yet." He leaned across the table and clasped her hand. She was so serious and so earnest in her endeavor to save him, he knew he could not dismiss her proposal lightly. He said softly, "Thank you, Clarissa. 'Tis generous of you to make such an offer, but unnecessary. I am quite content to wed Gillian."

"But Jane said—"

"Hush. Jane says a great many things, most of them nonsense." He released her hand and leaned back in his chair. "Even if I allowed you to make such a sacrifice, I still could not offer for Miss Beauclerk. Her father would never permit her to wed a penniless lord."

"You could elope. Miss Fenshaw told me one can be married over the anvil in Gretna Green."

"Who the deuce is Miss Fenshaw?"

"My governess. Mama turned her off last month."

"I am glad to hear it if she was putting such idiotic notions in your head. Elopement, my dear Clarissa, is behavior quite beyond the pale. No gentleman who truly cared for a lady would persuade her to elope."

He was about to ring for more tea when a footman tapped softly on the door, then stepped in, bearing several parcels. "I beg pardon, my lord, but these were just brought to the door, sent with Mr. Prescott's compliments. This large one is for Lady Clarissa."

Leo eyed the bulky package uneasily, but it was an elongated box, no more than a hand high, heavily wrapped and sealed. Relieved that it could not possibly contain a monkey, he watched his sister as her eyes lit with eager anticipation. "Go on and open it, minx."

Clarissa excitedly tore the wrappings off and lifted the lid. "Leo, do come look! 'Tis a bagatelle board. Oh, I do think Mr. Prescott the kindest person."

"How odd. I wonder what possessed him to give a well-bred young lady such a gift."

She flushed. "Tom Delacroix has one, and I did remark how much I liked it, but I promise you, Leo, I never hinted for one. Is it not lovely? Tom's is not nearly so nice," she said, running her hand caressingly over the red mahogany sides and across the clear glass cover. Unable to resist, she pulled the knob in the right-hand corner, then released it, sending a small round silver ball shooting forward. It careened off the tiny silver pegs and spun wildly before landing in a slot for thirty points.

"This one is for you, my lord," the footman said, placing a small box in front of him that bore the distinctive wrapping of Rundell and Bridges, Jewelers.

Leo opened the card. Prescott's hand was sprawling and as bold as the man himself. He read aloud, " 'I hope you will be pleased to accept this trifle that I send in gratitude for a most enjoyable evening. Your obedient servant, Oliver T. Prescott.' "

"Open it, Leo," Clarissa urged, momentarily abandoning

her bagatelle board to come lean over his shoulder. "Oh, I wonder what it can be."

He undid the wrapping slowly, then withdrew an exquisitely detailed silver snuffbox. On the ivory lid, two miniature figures were expertly captured in the opening steps of the quadrille.

"How very pretty," Clarissa cried, then teased, "Did you hint that you should like to have a new snuffbox?"

"No, I did not. I expect Gillian told him I have a collection, but this is far too valuable a piece to be passed off as a mere trifle." He expertly flipped the tiny catch with one hand, and the tiny hinge sprang open. "Well made, too, but I shall have to return it."

His sister's eyes lost some of their sparkle. "Must you? I think Mr. Prescott only meant to do something nice, and he has so much wealth, it cannot signify. He told me that it is false economy not to buy the best."

He snapped the lid shut and returned the trinket to its box. He could not explain to her that he already felt under a tremendous obligation to Prescott, or how galling it was to be indebted to a gentleman one did not particularly like and could never hope to repay. Leo was keenly aware that most of the servants in the house had been engaged at his future father-in-law's expense, with orders that all the tradesmen's bills were to be sent to him. The dinner last night, the breakfast this morning, were courtesy of Oliver T. Prescott.

"Leo, if you return the snuffbox, must I give back the bagatelle board?"

"You must do as your conscience dictates," he replied, rising abruptly. The new footman, whose name he could not remember, hovered at his elbow. "Yes, what is it?" Leo demanded with uncustomary impatience.

"There is more," he said, holding out two boxes. "These are for Lady Wrexham, and a large bouquet of flowers for her is in the hall, and a smaller one for Lady Clarissa, too."

"Flowers? For me?" Clarissa, who had never had anyone send her so much as a posy before, flew out of the dining room before her brother could stop her.

The footman coughed. "I understand her ladyship has taken to her bed. What should I do with these, my lord?"

Leo eyed the boxes. The larger one was from Fortnum and Mason's and was surely unexceptional—probably a box of chocolates. But the smaller one, like his, was from Rundell and Bridges. What would Prescott deem appropriate for Lady Wrexham? A garish diamond brooch or ring, perhaps? Whatever he had chosen, it was bound to be unsuitable—and expensive. Mere trumpery his mother would send back without a second thought, but if the piece were valuable . . . he knew she had an acquisitive nature. He sighed and ordered, "Send them up to Siddons. She will deal with them."

"Very good, my lord," the footman replied. He withdrew as Lady Clarissa danced back into the room, her arms full of flowers.

"Look, Leo, are they not lovely? I shall have to write Mr. Prescott at once and thank him. May I keep them in my room?"

The fragrant scent of pinks filled the room. They were pretty, but not nearly so much so as Clarissa, delight written wholly on her delicate face. It was as well, Leo thought, that Prescott could not see her at this moment. Likely he would fill the entire house with flowers.

Ashamed of his own ingratitude, he murmured, "Of course you may. Flowers are quite unexceptional."

"And the bagatelle board?"

"I suppose since Mr. Prescott is to be part of the family, an exception may be made, but Clarissa, I beg you not to . . . to get in the habit of looking for gifts from him. If there is something you desire greatly or need, I hope you will apply to me."

"But it looks closed," Gillian protested as they paused before the door of a small shop hidden in a corner of Piccadilly. It was a narrow building, the front unimpressive and situated well out of the fashionable area, where, Mrs. Ledbetter assured her, the nobility congregated.

"It is closed," Sir Harry replied, undisturbed, and rapped on the door with his cane. "No one but ourselves will be admitted today. I explained to Madame de Fleur the need for privacy, and she will see none of her regular clients while we are here."

"That is very kind of her to give up her custom, but do you think it necessary?"

Harry grinned thinking of the *demi monde* who frequented the establishment. His former mistress had run up a formidable bill, so much so that he had to break the connection, and every actress and ballerina of note craved a gown by de Fleur. Her work was exquisite. She was not merely an excellent modiste, but she designed her gowns to flatter her clients—and each was an original. He rapped impatiently on the door again and replied, "Perhaps not necessary, but we do not want rumors of our expedition to reach Leo, do we? Let us surprise him instead. As for Madame, you need not worry. I warned you, she is shockingly expensive and will charge you dearly for her time."

Gillian smiled. "Papa will be pleased. He is forever trying to persuade me to order some costly gown in the hope it will turn me into a beauty."

They heard the sound of a bolt drawn, then the door was thrown open. "Ah, my lord, *entrez, s'il vous plaît.* Quickly, quickly."

They were ushered into an elegant salon, and the door was thrown shut and rebolted behind them. Gillian gazed about her in astonishment. The room was lit by several crystal chandeliers, and their light reflected a dozen times over by the enormous mirrors hung on every wall. Chairs and love seats were strategically placed throughout the room, and delicately wrought screens partitioned off small alcoves. Every surface was draped with lengths of luscious silks, satins, and brocades.

Madame was tall, dark, extremely thin, and beautifully turned out. If the gown she wore was one of her own creations, she was also vastly talented. Waving her hands, the Frenchwoman hurried her new client to a circular dais toward the rear of the room, explaining, "Nothing can be accomplished until I have had a look at you. Sir Harry, assist her, please."

He obediently gave Gillian his arm, helping her up the three steps that circled the platform, then came to stand beside Madame de Fleur.

She put a quizzing glass to her eye, observed her client from head to toe, then walked slowly around the dais. Gillian, blushing, started to turn, but Madame ordered, "Stand still, *cherie*. I must be permitted to view you from every vantage point."

Silence reigned in the salon. Gillian tried not to fidget, but it was most embarrassing to be the center of such concentrated attention, particularly with Sir Harry watching.

At last the Frenchwoman returned to his side and tapped him on the arm with her fan. "*Tiens*! You ask the difficult. To turn the *jeune fille* into a lady of style, of elegance . . ." She shook her head.

Harry held out his hand to Gillian. "Come, Miss Prescott, we waste time."

The Frenchwoman laid a hand on his arm. "Do not be so hasty, sir. 'Tis difficult, but not, I think, impossible. Of course, it will be expensive, particularly so when you require the clothes at once."

Harry smiled. It was not he, after all, who would be footing the bills. "Mademoiselle's father will gladly pay whatever is necessary. Now, what of her hair?"

Madame de Fleur's perfectly shaped lips twisted into a pout of disapproval as she studied Gillian's crimped red curls, which framed her small face beneath a stylish but overly decorated bonnet. The Frenchwoman ordered the hat removed, observed her client anew, then sighed. "Dreadful, *n'est-ce pas*? But do not concern yourself, Sir Harry. Yvonne shall cut and style it herself." She picked up a small bell and rang it as she spoke.

"Cut my hair?" Gillian asked, her hand involuntarily reaching protectively toward her curls.

"You must trust Madame de Fleur," Harry told her. "The most beautiful women in Town are her clients." Which was true, even if they were not the sort one met in polite Society. He retired to a chair, stretched out his booted feet on a footstool, and accepted a glass of brandy from the maid who appeared at his elbow.

Across the room, Gillian was suddenly surrounded by a bevy of young women, all gowned in plain black bombazine. As Madame issued a stream of orders in rapid French, eager hands reached out to take her hat and reticule. Then she was swept up a steep narrow stair hidden behind one of the screens.

Harry bided his time, knowing it would be some hours before Miss Prescott would be returned to him. It was not the first time he had brought a customer to Madame, though he had never before brought a *respectable* young lady. He wondered what Leo would say, should he learn of it. No doubt he would disapprove. One could not blame him, for it was an outrageous scheme. Harry had protested himself when first his aunt proposed it—but it was also a brilliant plan. No one else in all of London could rig out a lady in prime style the way Madame could.

Harry grinned, thinking of his aunt. She was an amazing old lady. Why, he had never suspected she knew about de Fleur, but he should have known better. There was little in Town that escaped Aunt Seraphina's notice. It had even come to her attention that certain young ladies, friends of Miss Beauclerk's, had ridiculed Miss Prescott most unkindly, mocking her hair, her voice, her manners, and her style of dress.

For reasons Harry had never quite understood, his aunt had taken Miss Beauclerk into strong dislike. Well, he was not overly fond of the chit, either, and he had not looked forward to Leo's marriage to her. But that was far different than the open delight his aunt had expressed when she heard Leo was to wed Miss Prescott. She had instantly demanded to make the American's acquaintance and now seemed determined to make her all the vogue. Not that Harry minded. He rather liked little Miss Prescott. What he didn't like was deceiving his best friend. Aunt Seraphina had dismissed his notions as mawkish twaddle, declaring that Leo would one day thank him for his interference. Harry was not reassured.

When Leo called for Gillian as he was to escort her to a fashionable musicale this evening, he had his hands full trying to restrain Mr. Prescott's magnanimity. Leo had thanked him civilly for the gifts he'd sent, which were dismissed by Oliver as mere trumpery.

"Truth is, my lord, I was prepared to come down handsomely for Gillian's wedding, but with your family in mourning, 'tis going to be a paltry affair. So what I should like to do instead is refurbish your town house. Now, don't be offended, but I couldn't help notice that it has grown a bit threadbare. Why, the curtains and carpet in the drawing room must be half a century old if they're a day."

"Very likely," Leo replied evenly. "Your offer is extremely generous, but one which I must decline."

"Don't be hasty, my lord. I know my taste don't march with yours, and you're probably thinking I'd do it up in a way you wouldn't like, but think again. You and Gillian betwixt you may furnish it as you please and send the bills to me."

"It is not your taste I object to, sir, but needless expense. Once your daughter and I remove to Farthingale, I intend to put the town house on the market. So you see, it would be foolish to refurbish it."

Oliver was struck speechless for a moment, then protested, "But where will you stay when you come to Town?"

"We shall either lease a house or put up at Grillon's Hotel. Pray, do not look so shocked, sir. I assure you 'tis a very fashionable hotel. Even the King of France stayed there last year."

"Hmmph, that may be, but I don't take to the notion, no, nor see no rhyme or reason for it. You have no need to economize, my lord. I told you I would clear your mortgages, and if it's the staff you're thinking of, you may be certain I'll stand the nonsense, and gladly so, for I like to see my little girl living in style."

"Your generosity is . . ." *suffocating*, Leo thought, but smoothly changed it to ". . . overwhelming. However, I do not intend to be dependent on you, sir, and I believe you would not think well of me should I do so. Farthingale is a vast estate, and though it has been sadly neglected, it can be brought to pay for itself again. I mean to set it right—"

"What you mean is that Gillian will be stuck somewhere in the country and never see sight nor sound of Town," Oliver interrupted furiously. He rose to his feet, anger turning his face an unattractive red, and roared, "Your sister told me something of your precious Farthin-

116

gale—smoking chimneys and drafts strong enough to freeze a duck's tail, not to mention a leaking roof. That, my lord, is not what I had in mind for my daughter!"

"Then I suggest you find her another suitor," Leo replied, coming to his feet also. He was equally angry, but his voice was low and controlled. Only his eyes reflected the wrath he felt.

Oliver Prescott was stunned. Accustomed to dealing with lackeys who cowered whenever he raised his voice, it was a new experience to be met by a gentleman who seemed undaunted, and not a pleasant one. He stared at his future son-in-law, then muttered, "You don't mean that."

"Indeed I do," Leo replied calmly, his own temper now well in check. "Come now, sir, surely you do not wish a puppet for a son-in-law? The sort of frippery fellow who merely waits for you to pull the strings and willingly dances to your tune? I know a few such who would be more than happy to spend your money, and I can furnish you with an introduction . . . if that is truly what you wish."

"You know 'tis not, but demme, my lord, to think of my little girl living in an old barn of a place is more than I can bear."

Leo laughed at his soulful expression. "If you are basing your opinion on my sister's report, I must warn you that Clarissa is prone to exaggeration. Farthingale is in need of repair—and for that I shall not hesitate to draw on you—but I assure you it is quite habitable. Indeed, sir, I hope you will come stay with us and judge for yourself. And we shall come to Town on occasion. You must not think that I mean to keep Gillian a prisoner there, though I sincerely hope she will become as fond of the house as I am."

The door opened to admit Mrs. Ledbetter and Gillian. She was nervous as she faced the two men, but it did not

117

show in her bearing or her soft voice as she drawled, "Is it Farthingale you are speaking of, Leo? I confess, I am eager to see this house you hold so dear."

Both gentlemen swung around to greet her, and it was debatable which of the two was the more astonished by her appearance. The crimped curls that normally framed her face had been swept smoothly away from her brows and ears to repose in a pretty cluster at the back of her head. Her only hair ornament was a small cluster of white roses nestled against the curls. The style had the effect of making her eyes—easily her best feature— seem larger. Even her freckles seemed less prominent, although that was due to the tinted powder Madame de Fleur had provided.

Pearl drops accented her tiny ears, and a simple pearl necklace encircled her throat. Diamonds and emeralds, Madame had said, would be stunning after she was wed, but until then, nothing but pearls. Her gown, too, was simple and unadorned. Of white sarcenet over a slip of white satin, the dress was of moderate fullness and fell in a single sweep from her bodice to her ankles and was finished with a double braid down the center, of a color that matched her eyes.

White satin slippers peeped from beneath the hem of her gown, and long white gloves completed the ensemble. Madame had warned Gillian not to wear a shawl, for it would mar the clean lines of the gown, but she felt strangely exposed without one, the bodice was cut so extremely low. She waited nervously for the gentlemen to comment on her appearance.

Leo recovered first and came forward to bow gallantly over her hand. "My dear, you are in exceptional looks. Is that a new gown?"

"It is, just finished today," she replied, her eyes aglow as she read the approval in his. Then she turned to her father. "Papa, I hope you like it, too, for I must warn you, it was prodigiously expensive."

"Very pretty," he said, but his voice lacked conviction. "But is it not rather plain? Perhaps if you were to wear your diamonds, or the sapphires I bought you?"

"Precisely what I advised, sir," Mrs. Ledbetter said, nodding her head in agreement. "But our dear Gillian will not hear of anything but her pearls."

"I do not pretend to be conversant with fashions," Leo said, "but I believe pearls an excellent choice. Diamonds are certain to incite envy, and the gossipmongers will say she is flaunting her wealth."

"Well, what's the good of having 'em if she can't wear 'em?" Oliver demanded.

"It does seem unfair, does it not?" Leo replied, smiling. "But after Gillian is wed, she may wear all the jewels she pleases."

"Which no one will see if she's hidden away in the country," Oliver retorted, staring at his daughter. "What have you done to your hair?"

She crossed to him, stood on tiptoe, and kissed his cheek. "You sound unaccountably cross, Papa. I pray your foot is not troubling you?"

His anger evaporated as quickly as it had risen. With her hair drawn back, Gillian looked so very much like her mother. Fighting a wave of nostalgia, he caught her hand and squeezed it, saying gruffly, "And should I not be cross seeing my little girl grow up in a blink of the eye? Makes me feel my years, it does, but I shall do fine, puss. You run along with his lordship, and tomorrow I shall want to hear all about this grand party."

Lord Wrexham escorted the ladies to his waiting carriage, saw them comfortably seated, and when the barouche was underway, complimented Gillian again on how well she looked, before inquiring politely as to Mrs. Ledbetter's health.

Leo nodded politely as the older woman spoke, pretending an interest he did not feel. Although they had dined twice with Sir Harry's aunt, attended the theater and the opera, his mourning prevented him from appearing at all the balls and routs. The musicale this evening would be Gillian's real introduction to London's ton. Lady Jersey was hosting the affair, and one could be assured the cream of Society would be in attendance. Her invitations were much coveted, and he suspected his own was due to Lady Tyndale's influence. She was a descendant of the Childs, and a cousin, though several times removed, of Lady Jersey.

Their carriage slowed, but such was the traffic in the street, it was nearly a quarter of an hour before they were able to alight. Mrs. Ledbetter exclaimed at all the notable personages she recognized as they ascended the steps and joined the throng waiting to be announced. She prattled aimlessly, and the more she spoke, the quieter Gillian became.

Then it was their turn. Like being presented to royalty, Gillian thought, as she heard the butler announce their names in sonorous tones. Her hostess, looking very elegant in blue silk and diamonds, was receiving with her husband, the Earl of Jersey. He seemed quiet and rather dignified compared to the vivacious countess, who, true to her reputation, was never at a loss for words.

"Miss Prescott," she murmured, extending her hand, as her gaze roamed critically over her guest's attire. Finding nothing to fault, she said, "I have heard much of you from Lady Tyndale. But how naughty of you, my dear, to capture so handsome and charming a gentleman as Lord Wrexham when he has just returned to Town. The other young ladies will be positively green with envy. And you, my lord, why have you not called? Is it true your mother is in Town? Pray, give her my regards. Mrs. Ledbetter, charmed to meet you."

And then they were done, and admitted into the spacious drawing room, where chairs had been drawn into neat rows in preparation for the entertainment ahead. There were rumors that the popular new diva, Anna Maria Pavarotti, was to perform. At the far end of the drawing room, a beautifully detailed arch led into another salon, and that, too, appeared crowded.

Gillian looked at all the stylish ladies and gentlemen strolling about the room or standing in clusters. Very few were seated, but her own party had been a long time on the stairs, and then in the receiving line. She feared Leo's leg might be paining him and turned to ask if he wished to sit down. The question died on her lips.

Lord Wrexham, his countenance drawn and pale, stared across the room as a tall, blond, ethereal beauty entered. The girl paused in the archway and, as though she sensed his gaze, turned in his direction. Their eyes locked for a few brief seconds before the color drained from her face and she fainted.

"Diana," Leo whispered, his voice hoarse with agony.

Chapter 9

Lord Fenwick, entering the drawing room with Mrs. Beauclerk, saw the exchange of glances between Diana and Wrexham. With the lightning-fast reflexes that had earned him a reputation as a formidable fencer, he caught her in his arms as she swooned. Lifting her easily, he carried Diana back into the adjoining salon and placed her tenderly on a sofa near the windows.

Mrs. Beauclerk, looking extremely white herself, found a vial of smelling salts in her reticule and waved it beneath her daughter's nose. "Oh dear, I knew this would happen. It was inevitable that—"

"That the heat would overcome her?" Fenwick interrupted, his eyes warning the woman not to say what she was obviously thinking. He continued, "I am not surprised she fainted, madam. The heat in this room is stifling. Perhaps a window could be opened?"

As a footman leapt to do his bidding, Diana's eyes fluttered open. She noted the people clustered about them, Fenwick's concerned gaze, and her mother's worried frown. A faint tinge of color crept into her cheeks as she tried to sit up. "I am dreadfully sorry. . . ."

"Do not apologize, my dear," Fenwick said. "Neither your mother nor I was surprised that the heat overcame you, especially with the room so crowded. If you are sufficiently recovered, I suggest we step out onto the terrace. The cool air will do much to revive you."

"Thank you," she replied tremulously, and allowed him to assist her to her feet. She lifted her gaze and cast one quick look around the room, but the face she sought had disappeared, and others turned discreetly away.

"Diana, darling, are you certain you would not prefer to go home?" Mrs. Beauclerk asked solicitously.

It was of all things what she would have most wished, but Diana knew as well as Lord Fenwick that if she left now, the gossip would be far worse. She lifted her head and, summoning every ounce of her will, produced a smile. "Pray, Mama, do not make me leave. I will be better directly, and I do so much wish to hear Pavarotti sing."

Mrs. Beauclerk reluctantly agreed, and the curious parted to let Diana and Lord Fenwick pass through to the open door of the terrace. As they stepped outside, he smiled his approval. "Well done, my dear."

She lifted one of her delicate hands to her breast and bowed her head. Her voice throbbing dramatically, she refuted him. "No, my lord, 'twas not. To allow my emotions to overcome me in such a manner, to allow the world to see how my heart is breaking—I am so ashamed."

Vitalis, the Marquess of Fenwick, smiled indulgently. He was a good deal older than Miss Beauclerk, and he believed he understood her perfectly. At the moment, she fancied herself in love with Wrexham. She had confessed it was so when Vitalis first approached her, but all the same she had not spurned his own attentions. She craved adoration like a flower craves the light, and withered without it. He understood that, and he was quite prepared to adore her.

"I suppose it was the shock," Diana said. "I knew, of course, that I must sometime meet Wrexham, but I had not thought he would be here tonight . . . with her."

"Miss Prescott?" Fenwick questioned. "I know you

cannot look fondly upon her, my sweet, but, I vow, I pity her."

She turned a haughty shoulder to him. "You are more generous than I, my lord. Pray tell me why you should pity her."

"Is it not obvious? Everyone will. She is but a dab of a girl. The ton will naturally make comparisons, and poor Miss Prescott will suffer. She has not your beauty, or bearing, or wit."

Much struck, Diana considered the matter. "I only caught a glimpse of her, but I did not think her as ill looking as I had heard."

"She is presentable enough," he agreed, gently caressing Diana's shoulder as he turned her to face him. "But she cannot aspire to the beauty of the incomparable Miss Beauclerk. You, my sweet, are a diamond of the first water, and she but a pale little crystal."

Her lashes swept down. "I believe you flatter me, sir."

"Impossible, my dear Diana, when you are perfection itself. Why, when I look at you, the very air is suddenly filled with the sound of music."

She tapped him lightly on the arm with her fan as she laughed. "How absurd you are when you must know 'tis only someone playing the pianoforte. I apprehend the diva is nearly ready to perform. I suppose we should go inside, my lord."

"If you wish it," he replied, offering his arm while silently congratulating himself on his tactics.

In the long drawing room, Gillian pretended she was enjoying Pavarotti's singing as she sat stiffly beside Lord Wrexham. Her heart ached for him. How *crushing* to see the one person he most cherished not only set beyond his reach but dreadfully hurt by his own actions. And he was forced to behave as though nothing out of the ordinary had occurred. Gillian believed she was the only one to have seen the split second of agony in his eyes and the half step toward Miss Beauclerk before Leo restrained himself.

The sound of applause startled her, and she hastily joined with the others in clapping as Anna Maria Pavarotti bowed to her audience.

"Marvelous, is she not?" Leo asked.

"Indeed, yes," Mrs. Ledbetter replied. "We are privileged to have witnessed such a performance. Do you not agree, my dear?"

"She is most impressive," Gillian replied, but she was looking beyond Wrexham's shoulder to where Miss Beauclerk reposed on a settee near the door. A tall older gentleman, the one who had carried her from the room, danced attendance on the beautiful girl, along with a number of younger men, and several young ladies who were Miss Beauclerk's particular friends. Gillian felt a sharp pang of envy.

"Leo!" Sir Harry cried, coming up to them. "Thought I'd never find you in this crush. Miss Prescott, your servant." His eyes twinkled as he surveyed her, then added, "May I say you look exceptionally well this evening?"

"Thank you," she replied, feeling immeasurably better to have one friend in this crowded room. Gillian introduced him to her companion, and the conversation returned to the diva's performance. Sir Harry stayed talking to them for several moments, but though she responded appropriately, her thoughts were elsewhere. She could not help observing that Leo's eyes kept straying to Miss Beauclerk, and her ready sympathy enabled her easily to imagine the heartache he must be feeling. Determined to give him the opportunity at least to speak to Miss Beauclerk, she waited a moment, then remarked, "I feel as though I have been singing myself, so parched is my throat."

Leo bowed. "May I fetch you something cooling? Mrs. Ledbetter?"

"Perhaps a glass of orgeat," Gillian suggested, and tried not to feel hurt by the sudden eagerness she saw in his countenance.

As Leo walked away, Sir Harry, correctly reading her intention, murmured, "You have a kind heart, my dear, but I fear a foolish one. Must you dangle the carrot in front of the horse?"

She smiled wanly. "When it is what the horse so much desires, I feel I cannot but oblige. Moreover, sir, need I remind you that mine is to be a marriage of convenience?"

"I believe it could be otherwise, if you wished it . . . indeed, I suspect you are not entirely indifferent."

Mrs. Ledbetter demanded, "Indifferent to what? All this talk of horses and carrots—I declare you young people speak such nonsense, there is no understanding what you may mean by it."

"Sir Harry *is* talking nonsense," Gillian replied, though she could not help the faint blush that tinged her cheeks. "Now, do be serious, sir, and tell me how your aunt does."

"She is as tyrannical as ever, and sends her regards," he answered. "Shall we take a turn about the room?"

"Thank you, but no. I believe I shall seek the retiring room, if you will grant me leave."

"Do you wish my company, Gillian?" Mrs. Ledbetter asked. "If not, I shall just sit here, for my feet are aching terribly. I believe it must be coming on to rain, for they always do so when the weather turns wet. And someone should be here when dear Lord Wrexham returns with our refreshments. Gracious, he is taking an unconscionable time, is he not? Oh, I see, he has stopped to speak to that young lady. Do you know her, Sir Harry?"

Gillian left him to answer Mrs. Ledbetter, and, after receiving directions from a footman, started down the graceful curving stairs. Two young ladies, coming up, paused as she was about to pass by.

"Why, I believe it must be Miss Prescott," the taller of the two, her long, thin nose tilted high in the air, remarked to her companion.

Confused, Gillian looked at them. "I am sorry, have we met?"

"I am Miss Piedmont, and this is Miss Martin. We have not been introduced, but we are dear friends of Miss Beauclerk ... ah, I see you know the name. Naturally, we have heard much of you." She deliberately allowed her gaze to travel from the top of Miss Prescott's head to the satin slippers on her feet. Finding nothing to scorn, she smiled meanly, her small white teeth showing, then remarked, "How frightfully pleased you must be, to have your father buy Lord Wrexham for you."

Gillian gasped.

The short, slightly plump Miss Martin tittered. "La, Claudia, that is unkind of you ... true, but unkind." Laughing, the pair swept past.

Abovestairs, in a secluded alcove, Diana, her voice barely above a whisper, said, "I did not expect to meet you here tonight, my lord."

Leo stood before her, unconscious of how handsome he looked in his newly tailored black dress coat, unconscious of the crowded salon behind him, oblivious to everything save the hurt in her voice. He had been unable to resist the temptation to speak to her, to somehow reassure her. When he had seen her faint, it had taken all of his control not to come to her aid. But he knew he no longer had the right. Her words that she had not expected to meet him, and the insinuation that it was painful for her, cut deeply. Gravely he replied, "Nor I you. I saw Fenwick come in with you. Tell me, is it to be a match?"

Diana unfurled her fan and shrugged a pretty shoulder.

"I do not know, or why you should care. I will only say that he is very kind to me, and Mama would like it. If I wed him, I would be a marchioness, you know, and command every luxury."

"I did not think such considerations would weigh with you," Leo replied stiffly.

"No?" she retorted, stung by his unfairness. "And yet, am I not to congratulate you on making a most advantageous marriage? 'Tis said Miss Prescott's father is vastly wealthy."

"Diana, I—"

"Is it not odd?" she interrupted, her voice brittle. "I can recollect when first we pledged our love in the gardens at Farthingale. It was spring—do you recall, Leo? The sweet little forget-me-nots were just coming out, and the primrose was in bloom. In my mind, I can still picture it, almost smell the fragrance of the flowers. I was so happy then. I thought we would spend all our years together . . . but it was just a dream, was it not? Merely idle words. Oh, how vastly I was deceived!"

"Diana," he entreated. "You must know my . . . my feelings for you have not altered. You cannot blame me more than I do myself. If I had known the extent of my father's debts, or the position in which I now find myself, I never would have spoken."

"Then I am glad you did not know," she whispered passionately. "At least I may have the illusion that once you cared for me."

"Illusion?" he replied, as stricken as though she'd pierced his heart with a knife. "How can you say so when I have carried your image with me on every campaign, when I have prayed for promotion that I might be worthy of you? It was no illusion, Diana, and when I came home—" He broke off with a sigh. "Even now, if I thought there was the slightest change—but it is useless to speak of such. Your father would never permit us to marry."

"My father!" she echoed scornfully. She snapped the fan shut, and her eyes blazed with passion as she looked up at him. "Pray, Leo, do not blame my father for your lack of resolution. I would have wed you no matter what he said. Even if it meant we would have to live in a simple cottage—that would not have stopped me. I do not care what the world would say."

The sudden tears on her lashes affected him even more than her words. Leo wished he might take her in his arms and console her. Yet he knew he must not. He reminded himself that behind them, a roomful of people covertly watched and would relish the opportunity to gossip were he to take a misstep. Even as the thought entered his mind, he heard footsteps approaching and then Fenwick's deep voice.

"What is this, tears, my sweet? Because I left you so long? Come, my dear, I have returned, and brought you a glass of champagne." He handed her the glass, barely acknowledging Lord Wrexham's presence.

She took a sip and smiled bravely. "Thank you, Lord Fenwick. You are always so thoughtful, so considerate of my feelings."

"I ask nothing more of life than to serve you, my sweet," he replied, ignoring Wrexham's glare.

"Diana," Miss Piedmont called, rushing up to her. "You will never guess who I just saw! It was her—that dreadful Miss Prescott—" She broke off abruptly, perceiving Wrexham as he turned.

"The dowdiest thing," Miss Martin added, crowding in on her friend's heels. "And her voice! I do not know how Lord Wrexham can bear to listen to it—oh, 'tis you, my lord. I-I did not see you."

"I have the advantage," he replied curtly. "I recognized your voice before I turned. 'Tis such a *piercing* tone you have, but perhaps it merely sounds overly harsh to my ears after listening to Miss Prescott's soft drawl." Ignoring her look of outrage, he nodded to Fenwick, then bowed to Diana. "Obviously, I am *de trop*. Your servant, Miss Beauclerk."

Surprised by the sudden burst of rage he'd felt, Leo tried to dispassionately examine his anger while he procured two glasses of orgeat for the ladies of his party. Of course Diana was not to be blamed. Her unfortunate friendship with ladies of Miss Martin and Miss Piedmont's ilk was regrettable. She found the pair amusing and would not hear a word against them. It was not the first time Leo had been vexed by their presence. They were the worst sort of gossipmongers, and their chief form of amusement seemed to be finding fault with any young lady who had the misfortune not to be included in their particular circle of friends.

Like Gillian.

Could they not see that she had done nothing to deserve their ridicule? That he was in a position necessitating a marriage of convenience was not an offense that could be laid at her door. But Miss Piedmont was an intimate of Diana's and intensely loyal. She would take great pleasure in being uncivil to one whom she knew found no favor in her friend's eyes.

He threaded his way through the crowded room, once or twice detained by some well-wisher, then Gillian came into his view. She sat with her companion, the two quite apart from the press of other guests who chattered and circulated about them. No one approached the pair, no one stopped to speak a friendly word. Leo, his conscience reproaching him, apologized for the lengthy delay.

"Pray do not regard it, sir," Gillian said in her soft voice. "I have been exceptionally entertained. Mrs. Ledbetter has been pointing out all the notables present."

Was it only his imagination, he wondered, or was the color particularly high in her cheeks? He thought her eyes unusually bright, too, but he said only, "You are very kind to me, my dear, to be so forgiving when you should be scolding me instead. Now, would you like to take a stroll about the room? There are some friends of mine you might care to meet."

Gillian, who wished only to go home, shook her head. "I do not stand on ceremony with you, sir, and so will tell you frankly that I can see your leg is paining you. And, in truth, my head is aching a little. 'Tis dreadfully noisy here, is it not?"

"Lady Jersey's entertainments are always a squeeze," he agreed. "Do you really wish to leave, or are you only saying so because you think I should rest?"

When she had persuaded him she truly did not wish to remain, they took their leave of Lady Jersey. Mrs. Ledbetter was content and spent the carriage drive composing in her mind the letter she would write to her sister about the delightful musicale she had attended at the home of dear Lady Jersey. . . .

When they arrived at Cavendish Square, Leo escorted the ladies to the door. He was ready to bid them a good night when Gillian shyly asked him to step inside for a few moments as there was something she particularly wished to say to him.

He hesitated, and she cajoled softly, "I will not keep you long, my lord, and you need not fear encountering Papa, for he always retires early."

He glanced down at her, seeing the troubled look in her eyes and the way she held her slender shoulders so stiffly . . . poor little Gillian. She had struck a poor bargain, and he would not blame her if she meant to cry off. After giving his hat and gloves to Broom, he followed the ladies down the long hall to the drawing room. A footman opened the door for them, lit two of the candelabra, then silently withdrew.

"We shall not need you, Mrs. Ledbetter," Gillian said as they entered the room. "You may retire."

"But, my dear, merely because you are betrothed to his lordship does not mean you should entertain him alone. I am quite sure that—"

"What I have to say to his lordship is of an extremely private nature. Please leave us," Gillian interrupted. She waited impatiently by the door, tapping one slippered foot.

Leo listened to her in amazement. Her voice still held the gentle drawl he'd become accustomed to, but now there was steel beneath it. Like a fine sword wrapped in velvet, he thought.

When Mrs. Ledbetter was well away, Gillian turned to him with a rueful smile. "Pray forgive my plain speaking. I fear 'tis the only thing my companion understands." She gestured toward two chairs situated closely together. "Will you be seated, sir? There is a footstool if you wish to put your leg up."

"I am not quite an invalid," he replied, but he obligingly sat and stretched out his long legs.

Taking the chair opposite, she faced him squarely. "There are two things I wish to say to you. The first concerns Papa. I know he offended you earlier this evening—no, please do not disclaim," she said as he started to protest. "We have not been long acquainted, but I find I can sense when you are displeased, and I wish you will not dissemble with me."

Leo stirred uneasily. "If you will, then, 'tis true I was annoyed, but I think if I tried to explain it to you, I would sound like the most ungrateful creature alive. To take offense because someone is generous to an extreme . . . it sounds ludicrous, I know, but I feel as if . . . as if your father's generosity places me under an obligation I can never hope to repay. I know that is not his intention, but I would like him better if he did not try to do quite so much for me."

Gillian nodded. "I rather thought that was it, and I know it will do little good to tell you that Papa does not wish to be repaid. I shall try to restrain him. He so enjoys surprises."

"Like sending my sister a bagatelle board?"

She blushed slightly. "Do you dislike it? I know 'tis hardly a proper gift for a young girl, but she had mentioned how much she enjoyed playing one—"

He reached across and clasped her hand. "That I do not object to at all. Indeed, I am sorry he could not see how her face lit up when she opened the box. Nothing could have pleased her more, except perhaps the flowers he was thoughtful enough to send."

"I am glad," she replied, and then her lashes swept down as she asked hesitantly, "And the snuffbox?"

"I should return so expensive a gift—however, it is quite the nicest in my collection. Have you seen it? 'Tis beautifully wrought."

"Papa showed it to me," she confided, smiling a little. "I suggested it to him knowing you had a collection."

"You should not have done so, but thank you, my dear," he replied, lifting her hand to his lips and brushing a light kiss across her fingers.

She laughed. "Oh, perhaps you would have preferred a new and very stylish curricle? That is what he originally had in mind."

"Good Lord! Pray tell him how much I liked the snuffbox. Dare I ask what he chose for my mother?"

"Only a small brooch. 'Tis in the form of a peacock, but the . . . the bird's feathers are encrusted with gemstones." When Leo sighed and shook his head, she said, "It could have been worse, sir. He asked if I thought she would like a pair of peacocks, real ones I mean, for the lawn at Farthingale, since he had heard the Duchess of

Avon has such a pair. He thought they would make a very pretty picture spreading their plumage as they strutted across the terrace."

"I believe she would much prefer the brooch. In any event, she will not be long at Farthingale, you know. While we are on our wedding trip, my mother will remove to a small house in Bath."

"Must she?" Gillian asked. "I dislike the notion of putting her out of her home. She has lived there so long, she must be very fond of it."

"Not at all, so do not be thinking anything foolish. Indeed, I doubt she has ever liked the place. She has talked of removing for as long as I can remember. Which puts me in mind of something else. My aunt has a house in Hampshire and suggested we might like to stay there after our wedding. It's a very pretty little place, quite secluded. I would take you abroad, but with the situation so unsettled in France, I thought this might be preferable." When she did not respond immediately, he added, "Or if you prefer, we might visit one of the fashionable resorts."

She shook her head at that, the color rising in her cheeks. She had been conscious for some moments of her hand reposing in his, and now shyly withdrew it before saying firmly, "What I *would* like is to go immediately to Farthingale. It seems foolish to go on a wedding journey when ours is not the normal sort of marriage. What would you and I do in a secluded little house? And no one will be at Farthingale, will they, I mean, excepting servants? Your mother and sister will be in Bath, so it would give me a month or two to get sorted out before we have guests descend upon us."

"If that is what you wish," he agreed, trying not to show the reluctance he felt. "But you know we must return to Town in June. I've had an offer on the house here and that must be settled, and you will have your presentation at the Queen's Drawing Room. It hardly seems worth the trouble."

"We need not if you dislike the notion," she replied quietly. "I am sure Brighton or some other resort would be nice."

"Dislike it? No," he said swiftly. "But I suspect you are only saying that is what you would like because it would please me. If you are certain, then of course we may go to Farthingale." He could only pray that she would not be inclined to make many changes or find fault with his staff. Like the Craddocks, most of the servants were elderly retainers, people who had known him all his life.

As though reading his mind, she said, "You need not concern yourself that I will interfere overly much. After all, I shall only be there for a year or so, which brings me to the other matter I wished to discuss." She paused, swallowing over the sudden tightness of her throat. Then, staring straight ahead, she said, "I pray you will forgive me if I speak plainly about our situation."

"My dear, you need never guard your tongue with me."

"Then, let me say there is little point shamming it and pretending ours is anything but a marriage of convenience. We both know it, and what I wanted to say is that you needn't worry I shall be expecting you to dance attendance on me or account for every minute of your time. I won't be asking you what you've been doing or why you didn't come home for dinner." She glanced at him, the color high in her cheeks.

He smiled, his brows rising. "Gillian, I do believe you are giving me carte blanche to commence a career of profligacy. Do you expect me to offer you the same? I fear you will think me unhandsome for refusing to do so, but I will not. And furthermore, I shall reserve the right to ask you a great many questions, particularly if I notice you paying too much attention to other gentlemen!"

"That is most unlikely, and a different matter entirely. I shall, of course, try to behave as you think I ought, but I know that . . . that I am not the wife you wished for."

Leo rose, took the one short step that brought him to her chair, and drew her up. He knew there was no use trying to pretend it was not so, and he said gently, "Perhaps not, but all the same, I think I am most fortunate to have found you." He tilted up her chin and dropped a brief, warm kiss on her lips. "Most fortunate."

Chapter 10

Leopold August Thomas Reed and Miss Gillian Anne Prescott were married on the first of April in a very brief, very private ceremony. Because the groom's family was still in mourning, only a dozen or so guests were present. His elder sister, Lady Jane, and her husband were in attendance, and also Lady Barrows. She was Leo's aunt on his father's side, a high stickler, and something of a termagant. Lady Barrows disapproved of her sister-in-law, whom she disparaged as hen-witted, and had parted from her brother some months before his death on less than amiable terms. She had told him to his face that he was a wastrel likely to ruin the family, and his elder son a spendthrift lacking sufficient sense to come in out of the rain. Of Leopold, she knew little, but she was pleased by what she saw and held the opinion that he had acted just as he ought. Of his bride, she reserved judgment.

Clarissa, who acted as bridesmaid for Gillian, thought the ceremony terribly unromantic and decided that when she married, she would have an enormous wedding. She exchanged looks with Sir Harry as the bridal couple recited their vows. Her brother, she thought, was behaving magnificently. Only by his pale color would one guess that he was not marrying the bride of his choice. They made a handsome couple: he in his gray dress coat and Gillian in a deceptively simple white satin gown. Her hair was swept back in the new style she had adopted and crowned with a diamond-studded tiara from which a long, lacy veil fell over her shoulders and down her back. Gillian, looking as well as Clarissa ever had seen her, said her responses solemnly in her soft, drawling voice.

Lady Tyndale, who graced both the ceremony and the wedding breakfast, remarked to Lavinia, Lady Wrexham, that her new daughter was prettily behaved and would do very well. The father was regrettable, of course, but one must take the good with the bad.

"You may say so," Lavinia replied in throbbing accents. "But I will tell you that to see one's dearest son make such a noble sacrifice is almost more than one can bear. When I think of what might have been—but alas, you have never been a mother and cannot enter into such feelings."

"Do try not to be more of a ninnyhammer than you can help," Seraphina replied in her abrupt manner. "If you had the least pretension to good sense, you would see this is an excellent match for Leopold. Indeed, he has risen in my esteem for behaving so sensibly."

"Oh, what I would give to be blessed with your lack of sensitivity," Lavinia replied. "But 'tis my misfortune to feel deeply, and to see my dearest Leo, who has always behaved with the utmost thoughtfulness and considera-tion, who has been a tower of strength during my most trying times, to see him today under such circumstances as these—alas, I fear only a mother could partake of my sentiments—" She broke off, shaking her head sadly as she moved away.

Clarissa, who was standing nearby and overheard the exchange, bit her lip to keep from laughing aloud.

Sir Harry saw the merry look in Clarissa's eyes and grinned. "Lady Wrexham doing it too brown, is she?"

"You mean the *dowager*," Clarissa corrected in a low, mirthful voice. "I believe it is that which upsets Mama so much—and, of course, Papa Prescott."

"Am I to gather from such address that you are on intimate terms with him?"

She nodded. "Mama does not like it, but I think he is marvelous. He took me to Astley's last week, and he has promised I shall see the Tower of London when next I come to Town," Clarissa said, while wondering if her mother was sufficiently preoccupied with Leo not to notice if her youngest daughter drank a little of the champagne. She plucked a glass from a tray offered by one of a half dozen footmen circulating among the guests.

"Is that what you wish to do?" Harry asked curiously.

Clarissa laughed. "Visiting the tower may sound very tame to you, sir, but I find the prospect a vast improvement over spending the day sewing, or practicing the pianoforte. What is worse, we remove to Bath tomorrow, and there I shall be allowed only to accompany Mama to the pump room or the lending library."

"Is this chit complaining again?" Leo asked, coming up to them. "And what are you doing with champagne, my girl?"

"Papa Prescott said we were to drink a toast," she replied with a show of innocence.

"If you wish to toast our marriage, you may do so with lemonade," he informed her as he removed the glass from her hand. "Harry, make yourself useful, will you? Try to keep this minx out of trouble."

She made a face at his back as he walked away, then turned to Harry and complained, "I do wish Leo would realize that I am quite grown-up now. He treats me as though I were still consigned to the nursery."

Harry hid a smile. Clarissa had only emerged from the schoolroom last month, and she would not make her bow to Society until next spring. But all the same, she was not the little imp who chased after them when they were boys. With her hair up, and clad in a vastly becoming gray dress, she presented a pretty picture. He offered her his arm. "Then come, my lady, and let us take a turn about the room."

Gratified, she placed her hand on his arm in a most dignified manner, but a moment later she spoiled the effect with a giggle. "Harry, look. Papa Prescott is talking to Cecil, and I would give the moon to hear what he is saying. Oh, do let us go listen."

At the other end of the room, Gillian graciously accepted the felicitations of her few guests, smiled until the muscles of her mouth ached, and generally tried to behave as though she were not acutely conscious of her new married status. Sir Harry had bowed and called her my lady, and a number of others had greeted her as *my dear Lady Wrexham*. Gillian knew her mother-in-law had heard and did not appear pleased. The dowager behaved with civil, if chilly, cordiality, and had frequent recourse to her vinaigrette.

It was unfortunate, Gillian thought, that Leo's mother so much disliked the match, but at least his sisters had welcomed her to the family warmly and begged her to make use of their Christian names. And his aunt, Lady Barrows, had been an agreeable surprise. Apparently the marriage did have her approval, for she had announced that she would present the new Lady Wrexham at the Queen's Drawing Room in June, in place of Lady Tyndale, saying, "For though it was kind of Seraphina to offer, it should be a family member who sponsors you, my dear. And since Lavinia feels she is not well enough to do so, it falls to me to have that pleasant duty."

Gillian did wonder if Lady Barrows had behaved so kindly merely to spite her sister-in-law, for the two appeared to be at loggerheads. However, she had little time to worry over it. Her attention and concern were all for Leo. She saw that he was limping. Determined to leave as quickly as possible, Gillian slipped out of the room, hurried to her bedchamber, and changed into her traveling gown. Once on their journey, Leo would be able to drop the pretense that this marriage was what he desired.

Her reappearance was the signal for the guests to disperse, and Gillian saw to it that the leave-takings were not prolonged. Her father enfolded her in his arms, kissed her soundly, then symbolically placed her hand in Leo's, saying gruffly, "I know you will take good care of my little girl."

The dowager shed tears as she bid them good-bye and wished them well in such mournful tones that Leo laughed and reminded her they would be in Town again within two months. His sisters followed; Jane was perhaps subdued in her wishes, but Clarissa kissed Gillian's cheek, which won for her a grateful smile from her brother.

Sir Harry was the last of the guests and claimed for himself the privilege of escorting the bride to the waiting carriage. It stood at the door—a handsome new post chaise, with the Wrexham coat of arms emblazoned on the door, a pair of perfectly matched bay horses harnessed to it, and two liveried outriders. Behind it stood the fourgon that would follow with their baggage, Gillian's maid, and the earl's valet. It was an impressive sight, and Harry, taking it all in, grinned at Leo. "What, no footmen? Shabby, I call it."

Then Leo was inside, the steps put up, and the door shut. As the carriage swept out of the square, the guests stood outside waving their handkerchiefs and calling good-byes.

Gillian smiled and waved until they were out of sight, then leaned back against the cushions. "I declare, I never knew getting married could be quite so exhausting."

"Are you very tired?" Leo asked, his eyes warm with compassion.

"Not as much as I expect you are, and I hope that you

will not think you must entertain me. Pray, do put your head back and rest a bit."

Leo protested, but the sleeplessness he'd endured the night before, the strain of maintaining an untroubled countenance throughout the morning, and the gentle sway of the carriage combined to induce him to close his eyes. In a very short time, he was sleeping soundly, and Gillian did not awaken him until late that evening when they reached the posting house.

The following morning, Leo strode into the private parlor he'd reserved and found Gillian down before him. He paused in the doorway, observing her for a moment. She seemed engrossed in a novel and continued to read as she nibbled on a buttered scone. She looked quite pretty, he thought, noting the way the sun streaming in the window set her hair aglow. Fire and light . . .

Sensing his scrutiny, she glanced up, then shyly smiled. "I bid you good day, sir. I trust you slept well?"

"Like the dead," he declared ruefully as he crossed the room and took the chair opposite. "I believe I owe you an apology, my dear."

Her fair brows arched and the blue eyes held a hint of amusement. "Before breakfast? Tell me instead if you would prefer coffee or tea."

"Tea," he replied absently. "I half expected to find you angry with me, and if you were, I would not blame you in the least. Yet you do not seem at all disturbed. Can it be that you are unaware that it is customary for a gentleman to spend his wedding night with his bride?"

She prepared his tea for him, remembering that he liked it without lemon or cream and with one lump of sugar. She handed him the cup, then averted her eyes as she replied, "Do you not think it would be better to spend our first night as husband and wife at Farthingale, when we are both well rested?"

"Perhaps, but it was still unconscionable of me to leave you to sup alone. I swear I merely intended to rest for half an hour, no more. You should have ordered Thurston to wake me. Instead, I learned it was by your orders that he permitted me to sleep the night away."

"I hope you did not scold him for obeying me. We could both of us see how tired you looked." She did not mention that she had also seen how badly he was limping when they stepped down from the carriage, or the pain in his eyes that told her his head was aching badly.

"Married one day and already I am not master in my home," he said.

Her eyes flew to his, ready to apologize, then she saw he was teasing, and responded in kind. "Married one day and my husband chooses to mock me. However, you may make amends by eating the breakfast I ordered for you." She smiled at him as the innkeeper entered carrying a large tray and began to set out various dishes.

"Gillian! I cannot possibly eat all this."

"Then take only what pleases you," she suggested, and discreetly watched to see what tempted him. She knew he had very nice tastes, and if his food was not served just so, he would eat very little. She hoped the cook at Farthingale was competent, which put her in mind of something else. "Your valet said we will reach Farthingale late today. Would you tell me something about the house and what I may expect?"

He told her a little, but mostly of the village. "The house you shall have to judge for yourself. I find I am not very good at describing it," he said when she pressed him for details. He knew from past experience that one either loved it on sight or despised it.

"Is it very large?" she asked a little apprehensively. She had managed Willowglen for several years, but she had had the aid of a considerable staff, and the house had been built when she was a child, so it was in excellent

143

condition. Farthingale, she knew, was erected in the early sixteen hundreds, and added on to by successive generations of Reeds.

"Not like Blenheim or Oatley Park," he assured her, knowing she had visited those stately homes. In his mind, it was much nicer, much more comfortable, but not everyone shared his opinion. His mother had never liked the house, and Jane, though she was fond of the place, much preferred her own neat little house with all its modern conveniences.

Gillian drew him out to talk of his staff. She had met Thurston, of course, and there was Partridge, the elderly butler who had been at Farthingale for as long as Leo could recall. And Mrs. Sewell, the housekeeper, who had replaced Mrs. Craddock when she became too enfeebled to run the house, and a dozen others whose names and histories he rattled off with ease.

Their conversation continued in the carriage when they'd departed the inn. But although Gillian plied him with questions, she was still unprepared for the beauty that met her eyes when they drove across the wold late that afternoon. Low stone drywalls enclosed lush green fields, where hundreds of black-faced lambs romped on their thin little legs. The road was built of yellowish Cotswold stone, Leo told her, and he couldn't keep the pride out of his voice.

"How lovely," she murmured, admiring the fruit trees that were in bloom—pear and plum, and delicate pink peach blossoms. This was very different from London with its chilling fog and dirty, noisy streets. Here the hedgerows were newly green, and the chestnut and poplar trees were beginning to acquire their spring cloak of new leaves, providing shade for the wood anemones and daffodils that grew beneath them. Alongside the road, primroses bloomed, and over it all fell the golden rays of the setting sun.

They crossed a stone bridge with a triple arch, and from the carriage window Gillian could see trout swimming lazily on the gravelly bottom of the clear stream. Above, on the grassy banks, a family of white ducks paraded toward the water. The carriage swept onward toward the village, and here she saw the weathered gray stone houses that lined both sides of the broad curving street. Ivy surrounded the rows of mullioned windows, running up to the oddly placed gables in the steep slate roofs. Forget-me-nots bloomed near the doors, and window boxes were bright with color.

"Almost home," Leo said quietly, but Gillian sensed an impatience and excitement within him.

A few miles beyond the village, the carriage turned left, entering a wide avenue bordered by chestnut trees, their branches arching above and across until they nearly met. Then she caught sight of the house.

It was perhaps the best time of day to see it. Built of gray Cotswold stone that had mellowed through the years to a soft golden glow, Farthingale looked as though it were bathed in sunlight—and as though it had sat there for hundreds of years. Even the new wings, which Leo had described, were indiscernible from the old, except perhaps the mullioned windows were larger. But all the gray slate roofs sloped steeply down from simple, narrow chimneys, and all the gables had the same sharp design.

On the left, the lawn ran down to the primrose-covered banks of a wide stream overhung with chestnut trees. To the right were hedgerows, and beyond them Gillian could see the start of a formal garden. At first glance, it was picturesque and her heart leapt at the sight of it. Perhaps it was her mother's blood stirring in her veins, but she had the oddest sensation that she had come *home*.

Farthingale was a house to love, to cherish—but it had been sadly neglected. Her keen eyes noted the weeds choking the drive, the overgrown flower beds, the lawn

145

that needed cutting, and windows so grime-laden she doubted one could see the view.

She said nothing as Leo helped her down from the carriage and escorted her to the door. It was opened promptly by a stately butler in neat, if faded, livery. She saw the old man's affection for Leo as he bowed them into the hall, where the rest of the staff was lined up and waiting to greet their new mistress.

Gillian walked beside her husband down the length of the hall, saying a few words to each of the servants, noting how easily Leo spoke to them and inquired after their various families. She paid particular attention to Mrs. Sewell. The housekeeper was a tall woman, neither fat nor thin, and with her gray hair and lined face looked to be as weathered as the house itself. Her tone was polite, her manner deferential as she curtsied, but Gillian sensed the woman was taking her measure and would not give her allegiance to her new mistress easily.

Cook, the two parlor maids, the footmen, and the kitchen maids all welcomed her warmly, but she felt that they, too, were waiting to pass judgment, or perhaps they were merely taking their cue from the housekeeper.

Tea had been laid in the south drawing room, Partridge told her when the staff was dismissed, unless my lady wished to be shown to her room. Gillian replied tea would be lovely. Her throat was quite dry after the dusty drive. She put off her pelisse and gave it with her hat and gloves into the butler's care, then followed one of the parlor maids—either Minna or Freda—up the broad oak staircase.

The drawing room was in one of the new wings, and Gillian saw immediately how beautiful it could be. Large and well lit by windows on two walls, the west side contained a charming bay and the north wall an enormous fireplace with an oak overmantel. The worn brocade window hangings and upholstery were a dark rose, and the carpet threadbare. But one hardly noticed. Heraldic shields of stained glass were set into the upper portions of the bay window, and the setting sun shining through it produced tiny rainbows all the way across the floor.

Gillian smiled with delight as Leo seated her in one of the comfortable chairs drawn near the warmth of the fire. "I begin to perceive why you are so fond of this house."

He breathed a sigh of relief, not even aware that he had been anxiously awaiting her judgment. And perhaps because she did not criticize his beloved Farthingale or complain of how shabby it appeared, he said, "I know there is much work to be done, but for so long we could not afford even the most minor of repairs. However, with the proceeds from the town house—did I tell you Halthorpe was able to sell it for well above what I expected?—yes, well, now I can begin to make some much-needed repairs."

"The rooms are beautifully proportioned," she commented as she prepared his tea. "It will be most pleasant to sit here in the afternoons." And silently she vowed to have a lengthy discussion with Mrs. Sewell. A lack of funds was not sufficient excuse for the dust that had accumulated, the lack of polish on the wood mantel, or the slightly tarnished silver that graced the table.

"When you're done with your tea, I will take you up and show you our bedchambers. Then tomorrow Mrs. Sewell can take you about and answer any questions you have about the household. I . . . I hope you will find her agreeable. Like most of the staff, she has been at Farthingale since I was a boy."

"She seems most amiable," Gillian said, blushing slightly because she knew he was politely telling her not to meddle. The reminder was well timed. Her mind had been busy with plans for improving the house. The oddity of being married, having breakfast with her husband, and being introduced to his staff, had nearly made her forget that theirs was, after all, but a temporary arrangement. In a year or so, she would return to Willowglen. She knew it behooved her to bear that in mind.

Leo saw her tale-telling blush, but he thought it was because he had mentioned the bedchambers. He knew he would have to be very patient and very gentle with his bride. His amorous liaisons in the past had been with experienced women, members of the *demi monde*, actresses . . . women who wanted only a pretense of affection and expensive gifts in exchange for their favors. With Gillian, it would be vastly different.

Gillian stood at the casement window of her bedchamber and looked out at the lawn. By starlight, it was quite beautiful, for one could not see all its imperfections. She hoped the same would hold true for her when Leo came. She turned back, observing the room now dimly lit by the fire burning in the hearth and one branch of candles. The huge four-poster bed dominated the room. The bed to which every Earl of Wrexham brought his bride, the bed where Leo was conceived.

She thought of her mother-in-law who had borne four children, of the maid at Willowglen who had become with child . . . surely it could not be so difficult? Surely there was nothing to be frightened of . . . but still the blood in her veins raced wildly and her heart pounded. She crossed to the small table near the bed and picked up her glass, drinking deeply. Leo had suggested they share a bottle of wine, that it would ease her nervousness—but it didn't. The wine only made her feel light-headed and a trifle warm.

She wondered if she should be in bed when he came, if that would not be less awkward. A pity there was not an instruction book for new brides, she thought. It was not knowing precisely what to expect that made her so apprehensive. She remembered again Mrs. Ledbetter's discussion with her the night before the wedding. Her companion had come to her room, she said, to warn Gillian of what she might expect.

"You must understand, my dear, that 'tis a wife's duty to accommodate her husband's, uh, passions. There are some—I will not say ladies—but some females who actually seem to derive some enjoyment from *coupling*, but I fear that ladies of sensitive natures and refined tastes, such as ourselves, must always find it rather unpleasant. I shall advise you as my mother did me: When your husband comes to your bed, keep your eyes closed and try to turn your mind to more agreeable thoughts."

"I am not sure I understand what . . . what happens," Gillian had ventured, her face flaming.

"You need not," Mrs. Ledbetter replied, her own face quite red as she rose and walked to the door. "Your husband will do all that is necessary. Just . . . lie still and allow him to have his way with you, then it will be quickly over."

Recalling her companion's words did nothing to reassure Gillian. She would have fled the room were it not for the tantalizing memory of Leo's kisses, which he had said were a mere prelude to what followed. His kisses had not been at all unpleasant. Indeed, she had quite enjoyed the way he made her feel. An impish grin tugged at the corners of her mouth. Perhaps she had not as much sensibility or refined taste as Mrs. Ledbetter thought.

A light tap on the door leading to the adjoining room sent her thoughts skittering and the blood rushing to her face. Panicked, her eyes desperately searched for a place to hide, but before she could move, Leo stepped through the door. Her first thought was how handsome he appeared; her second, the realization that he wore only a brocade dressing gown. She had never seen a gentleman so scantily clad before. She stared, forgetting that she herself wore just a thin white chemise and wrapper.

Leo saw the vulnerability in her eyes, knew intuitively that she would take flight if he made one false step. She was like a deer, suddenly aware of the hunter. He smiled, casually bid her a good evening as though this were an ordinary occasion, then said softly, "I do not believe I have ever seen this room look so lovely."

His words broke the spell she seemed to be under. She glanced about the bedchamber. "I suppose 'tis the candlelight."

"I rather think 'tis the mistress," he replied as he reached her side. He took her hand in his and found it trembling. "Do not be alarmed, Gillian. I promise I shall do nothing you dislike."

"I . . . I fear I am a little nervous," she confessed. "I have never done anything like this before."

He laughed aloud. "Lord, I should hope not. Come, my dear."

He led her—not to the bed as she had thought he meant to do—but to the love seat positioned near the fire. "Let us sit and drink some wine, and talk a bit. Would you like that?"

She nodded shyly, allowed him to position a cushion behind her back, and watched as he crossed the room to fetch the wine and glasses. He moved gracefully, but she could see the muscles rippling in his back beneath his dressing gown. Strangely, she found the sight more exciting than frightening.

He poured her a glass of wine and offered it as he sat down beside her—very close beside her. "Are you not having any?" she asked.

"I shall. Have you tasted the wine? It is a very old Bordeaux that has been in our cellars for years, a wine that the Wrexhams reserve for the most special of occasions."

As he spoke, his hand lifted a curl that danced against her shoulder, and he wound it around his fingers.

His touch made her skin tingle. She tried to concentrate on what he was saying. She *had* sampled the wine but could not have said if it was white or red, or sweet or tart. Beneath his eyes, sitting so closely beside him she could feel the heat from his body, she took another sip. "I . . . 'tis very good."

"May I?" he said, and before she realized his intent, he bent his head and tasted the wine on her lips. His touch was brief, light, and gone before she had time to take fright. He smiled down at her. "Delectable, delicious, and highly desirable."

"I am sure 'tis an excellent vintage," she murmured, mesmerized by his eyes. He had incredibly thick lashes. . . .

"I was not speaking of the wine," he answered, his voice low. This time his hand crept down her neck to beneath her chin, and gently lifted her face. His lips brushed hers tenderly, then more insistently.

Gillian closed her eyes, reveling in the warm, pleasurable sensations he evoked. This was not disagreeable at all . . . she nestled against his broad shoulders, the tense muscles in her neck and back relaxing beneath his soothing hands.

Leo lifted his head, then dropped featherlight kisses on her brow and her nose. He had to suppress the sudden surge of desire he felt. Patience, he reminded himself. "More wine, my dear?"

Gillian giggled. "I fear if I drink any more, I shall not be able to walk to our bed."

"Then I shall carry you," Leo promised, and when her glass was empty, the fire burned low in the hearth, and her eyes grown warm with desire, he kept his word.

Chapter 11

Gillian blushed a great deal in the months that followed. Contrary to Mrs. Ledbetter's expectations, she discovered that she was one of those females who quite enjoyed *coupling*. Her husband seemed to take his duty to produce an heir very seriously, seducing his wife at the most inopportune times, and teasing her with innuendos and pointed remarks over the breakfast or dinner table.

"What will the servants think?" she scolded him one morning when they had remained in her bedchamber exceptionally late. She scrambled into her clothes, too embarrassed to admit even Lucy to the room.

"I suppose they will think I am a very fortunate fellow," he replied, kissing the nape of her neck instead of hooking the buttons of her day dress, as she had directed him to. "Do you really care?"

"Leo, we must set a good example," she said, trying to suppress the delightful sensations she felt whenever he touched her. She turned in his arms to remonstrate, with the result that he kissed her upturned nose and then her lips, and it was nearly noon before they appeared in the breakfast parlor. No one said a word, of course, but the servants *looked* at her in such a manner that Gillian felt very certain they knew precisely how she had spent her morning. She tried to explain that to her husband, but all Leo would say was that he thought her quite adorable when she blushed.

In truth, her very obvious affection for the earl did much to reconcile her presence to the servants. They had not been inclined to accept an American as mistress, and the dowager's remarks about her father, and the fact that he was in trade, had been a black mark against her before she ever stepped foot inside Farthingale. Lavinia had also allowed it be known that her son's marriage was one of convenience only, and that Leopold would never have looked at such a girl were it not for her father's vast wealth.

From Partridge, to Mrs. Sewell, down to the scullery maids, the staff treated her with icy politeness. They were never disrespectful, never refused to follow her orders, but any changes Gillian suggested were inevitably met with the response, "Yes, my lady, but let us see what the master says."

As Leo, when applied to, invariably answered that household affairs were not his concern and any decision must rest with Lady Wrexham, the staff very quickly gave up that strategy. They discussed Gillian in the servants' hall, and it was agreed she was not a grand lady like the dowager, nor easy in her manner like the earl. They continued to carry out her orders, but with maddening slowness.

Gillian waited a week. Cook was her first priority. She had noticed at once that Leo barely touched his food, and she could not blame him. Their meals were frequently served cold, the meat not always thoroughly cooked, and the breads still doughy in the center. She sent for Cook on a Tuesday morning when Leo had ridden out to visit his tenants. Dismissing Lucy, Gillian sat behind the antique oak desk in her private sitting room.

Mrs. Mullins, though no one ever addressed her as anything but Cook, stood before her mistress with an air of defiance. She was plump, and Gillian noticed the black dress she wore was shiny and stretched thin in places.

Her mobcap might once have been white, but now it was yellowed with age, as was her apron. Gillian studied her for a moment without speaking.

Mrs. Mullins shifted nervously, but her mouth was set in a stubborn line and she avoided looking directly at Lady Wrexham.

"Cook, I asked to speak with you privately because I am concerned about his lordship. I understand you have been in charge of the kitchens for nearly twenty years."

The round brown eyes came up to regard her warily. "Yes, my lady."

"Then may I assume that you have a fondness for my husband?"

"Yes, my lady."

"Good," Gillian replied, smiling. "I will tell you in confidence that I am worried. His lordship's appetite is not what it should be since he was wounded. Have you noticed that he hardly touches his food?"

"Yes, my lady, but the master ain't never been a big eater, not like his papa or his brother, who betwixt them could clear the table, and often did. No one never complained of my cooking," she added, somewhat defensively.

"I am sure they did not, but his lordship is very particular, and I think we must make an extraordinary effort to tempt him to his food. Now, I have noticed that dinner is not served as warm as it should be, and that frequently the bread is not cooked through."

"That ain't my fault, my lady," Cook replied quickly. "You saw that old oven we got in the kitchen and—"

"I am not here to lay blame," Gillian interrupted in her soft drawl. "What I wish to know is what we may do to rectify the situation. If the oven is not functioning efficiently, then it must be replaced, as well as anything else in the kitchens that is outmoded or in need of repairs."

Cook's eyes lit with anticipation. For years now she had been hearing about the new Bodley closed range used by her sister, who was cook for a well-to-do gentleman and his lady, and had coveted it greatly. She tentatively suggested the new stove, adding, "My sister says it's ever so much more economical, my lady, as it burns less fuel."

"Then, by all means, let us have the Bodley. I shall arrange it. I expect you will require more help as well. Let me have a complete list, if you please, of what you feel would be an adequate kitchen staff. Now, as to menus. I have noticed his lordship is particularly partial to lamb. I thought for dinner we could have that with a nice mint sauce—is there a problem?"

"I am sorry, my lady, but there's no lamb in the storehouse." For once, Cook sounded truly regretful.

"Then you must order some. Be sure to include on your list all the supplies you need. We cannot scrimp when it comes to his lordship's health."

"Yes, my lady," Cook replied, a zealous gleam in her eyes. "I'll get started on it right away." She curtsied and hurried to the door, but paused there. "We have some strawberries, my lady, from the greenhouse. I recollect the master was fond of them when he was a lad. Do you think he would fancy some tarts with his dinner?"

"I think he would be well pleased," Gillian replied, more than a little pleased herself.

Cook's capitulation was complete a few days later when a seamstress arrived to take measurements for new uniforms for all the kitchen staff. She sat in the servants' hall that evening and remarked to Mrs. Sewell, "Say what you will, I think the master did well in bringing my lady to Farthingale."

Mrs. Sewell said a great deal, most of it uncomplimentary to Lady Wrexham. The housekeeper had long grown accustomed to blaming the lack of help for the disreputable state of the house, and Gillian had been unable to completely hide her disgust with such excuses. She would have polished the wood herself and cleaned the windows rather than let the household fall into such a neglectful state.

New uniforms did not pacify Mrs. Sewell, nor did the addition of several maids. Gillian tried to be tactful, but when she came into the breakfast parlor and saw dust on the table, or the silver tarnished, she grew impatient and spoke more sharply than she intended.

Mrs. Sewell, who knew herself to be at fault but loathe to own it, resented what she considered to be the usurpation of her authority. Lady Wrexham frequently gave orders directly to the maids instead of laying her complaints, as was proper, with the housekeeper. The dowager had never complained of her laxness, had willingly accepted the excuse of insufficient help, and turned a blind eye to the laziness of the staff. Matters came to a head a week later when Mrs. Sewell found two of the maids turning out the south drawing room, ordered to do so, they said, by Lady Wrexham.

The housekeeper sought Gillian out in her sitting room, and when admitted, said stiffly, "I beg your pardon, my lady, but if you wished the drawing room turned out, I would have seen to it had you told me so."

Gillian resisted the temptation to reply that she wanted it done properly and said only, "Yes, well, you were occupied with other matters."

"My lady, I cannot run the household properly if you are going to be giving orders to the staff without my knowledge." Her tone was defiant, her manner challenging.

Gillian rose behind her desk. Her voice was still soft, but beneath it was steel, cutting and sharp. "I regret you feel that way, Mrs. Sewell, but if you were running the house properly, it would not be necessary for me to interfere."

Neither woman was aware that Leo had returned early and seeking his wife, had stepped quietly into the room.

He was appalled to hear the housekeeper addressing Gillian in such a manner and crossed the room quickly to stand by his wife's side.

"My lord, I didn't hear you come in," Mrs. Sewell said, dropping a swift curtsy and smiling warmly at him.

Leo controlled his anger; his tone was civil, but his words for all the quiet tone lashed with the sting of a whip. "Mrs. Sewell, you have been at Farthingale for as long as I can recollect. I have always considered you something of an old friend and find it distressing that you have so little respect for the lady I have chosen to be my wife, and consequently for myself. I cannot and will not tolerate such conduct. If I should ever have occasion to hear you address her ladyship in such a manner again, you will be turned off at once and without references."

Mrs. Sewell swallowed. Even under the new Lady Wrexham's firm rule, she had a comfortable position and knew it would be difficult to find another. Bobbing her head, she said meekly, "I am sure I am very sorry, my lord. My lady, I never meant no disrespect."

"Thank you, Mrs. Sewell, that will be all," Gillian answered. And when the housekeeper had disappeared, she turned to her husband with a rueful smile. "I suppose I should apologize, too, but I *have* tried to deal with her tactfully."

He leaned down and kissed her brow. "My dear, you have nothing to apologize for. If anyone is remiss, 'tis I for not making it clear to the servants that your authority was absolute. You may be sure the word will quickly spread now, but should you have any further problems, do not hesitate to dismiss anyone who troubles you."

"Thank you, but I know it would distress you were I to do so."

"Not nearly as much as it distresses me to see you disturbed. Servants can be replaced, my dear, but not my wife."

She hugged his words to her. Perhaps they were casually spoken, perhaps he did not even mean what he said, but all the same the knowledge that he held her in such high regard warmed her heart.

The household at Farthingale prospered as the end of the following month drew near. The rooms had, one at a time, been thoroughly turned out. The windows now shone clearly, the furniture and woodwork glowed. The tables and sideboards that had appeared dull because of years of accumulated wax now glistened. Gillian had shown Mrs. Sewell how to remove the old wax with flannel soaked in beer, before applying fresh beeswax and turpentine.

The servants felt a resurgence of pride. They, too, had been turned out and looked fresh and smart in their new uniforms and livery. Not a piece of furniture had been replaced or moved at Farthingale; nothing had basically changed, and yet everything was different. Her household running efficiently, Gillian began to lay plans to replace the faded brocade curtains and tattered chair covers. Not with new designs. She hoped to duplicate the original patterns.

She was in her sitting room looking at samples of material when Leo sought her out one afternoon. She immediately laid aside her work, begged him to be seated and put his feet up.

"You will spoil me," he warned her, but he rather enjoyed her pampering. No one had ever been quite so concerned about him, quite so attentive to his needs. He had not expected to enjoy his marriage to Gillian. She was not the woman he'd loved for so many years, but a quiet affection had sprung up between them. He had delighted in teaching her the fine art of *coupling*, as she called it, and she was an apt pupil. But it was more than that. Gillian shared his sense of humor, she was always ready to enter into his plans for Farthingale, and she put forth many practical suggestions.

He studied her as she sat beside him, and realized what he had found was contentment—and he was loathe to disrupt it.

"What troubles you, Leo, that you must frown so?" she asked with wifely concern. "I know 'tis not the new sheep, for Halthorpe told me they are doing splendidly, nor the tenants. Except for Mrs. Craddock, they are all well, and even she is doing better since she began taking the tonic Dr. Westcot prescribed."

"For which she has you to thank," he acknowledged. Gillian did not dispense largess with an open hand as his mother had whenever the dibs were in tune, but she did care about the tenant farmers, and she saw that they had what they required. They did not adore her as they did the dowager, but they gave her their respect.

"Which still does not tell me what is troubling you," she prodded gently when he said nothing further.

"Nothing of any moment, just that I fear 'tis time we returned to London, and, very selfishly, I am reluctant to remove. There is still so much to do here, but it will keep."

"Must we go?" she asked, as disinclined as he to disturb their idyll. "Can we not send letters to everyone and say we intend to remain fixed at Farthingale?"

His brows rose, and his mouth quirked at one corner. "I think not, my dear. Somehow I doubt Her Majesty would understand were you to decline to attend her drawing room. And I shudder to imagine what my aunt would have to say."

"Oh, bother, I had quite forgotten my presentation. But surely we need not stay in Town long?"

"I think a fortnight, at least. Your father will wish to see you, and if you should not dislike the scheme, I thought to bring Clarissa to stay with us. I believe she is having a miserable time of it in Bath."

Gillian nodded. "I had a sweet letter from her. She offered, should Papa miss me too greatly, to allow him to adopt her. She rather thinks she would enjoy being an only child."

"She would, indeed, the minx, particularly if her father was the wealthy Oliver Prescott, and much inclined to indulge her whims. I cannot think how you turned out so well, my dear."

Gillian's blue eyes reflected her amusement, and Leo, realizing what he had said, colored a little and beat a hasty retreat. "I did not mean to imply that your father is—"

She laughed aloud. "What a bouncer. You most certainly did, and he most certainly is." Mischief danced in her eyes as she added, "I could, of course, return the compliment to your mother."

"Wretched girl, how dare you mock me?" he teased. "I shall—" He broke off as he saw her suddenly grimace. "Gillian, my dear, are you in pain?"

She shook her head, but the color had receded from her face, so her freckles were pronounced, and she bit her lip. After a moment, she appeared better and told him, "No doubt I should not have eaten those green apples in the orchard this morning. I have been feeling a little bilious all the day, but I am sure 'tis nothing."

"All the same, I think you should have Dr. Westcot in tomorrow. Promise me you will."

Touched by the concern she saw in his eyes, she replied that if she was not feeling better, she certainly would. But Gillian hated what she called fuss as much as her husband, and she did not feel sufficiently ill to seek out the doctor. The unpleasantness she'd experienced passed, though it recurred now and again in the days that followed. Gillian blamed it on the green apples and knew she should cease eating them—but she could not resist the temptation. Bad for her they might be, but she craved them at odd times, and nothing else seemed to satisfy her.

Gillian was duly presented at court in a wide-hoop gown of pale green silk and a towering headdress of dyed ostrich feathers. The dress had to be let out, for she'd had it fitted before their departure for Farthingale and on her return to Town discovered that she had since gained a few pounds. Leo teased her and said 'twas obvious married life agreed with her, and begged her not to try a reducing regimen.

She, however, thought she looked ridiculous, and had never felt more uncomfortable than in the tight-fitting gown and awkward hoops. But her father declared he thought her handsome, and Lady Barrows said in her terse way that she would do, and later remarked to a friend that Lady Wrexham might be the daughter of a cit, but the family need not blush for her manners.

And when the Wrexhams visited in Cavendish Square the following morning, Oliver Prescott demanded to hear all the particulars again, even though Gillian had recounted every detail to him the evening before. He swelled with visible pride as he listened, then said roughly, "I only regret your mama's not alive to see this day, puss, for though she had her heart set on you marrying a proper English gentleman, I don't expect she looked so high as to see you hobnobbing with royalty."

Everything taken into consideration, Leo felt their visit to Town was progressing better than he had expected. He was in such charity with his father-in-law that he met Oliver's generous offer to renovate Farthingale with gas lighting with good humor. He refused, of course, as he refused the gift of a china dinner service, gold-rimmed, which would accommodate four and twenty.

"But you must allow me to give you something, my lord," Oliver insisted when Gillian left them alone for a few moments. "Seeing my little girl making her bow to royalty—well, I don't hesitate to tell you it was the greatest moment of my life. And it's you I have to thank for it."

"My dear sir, you have already given me a gift of inestimable value for which I shall forever be indebted to you."

"If you mean the mortgages or that painting—"

"Not at all," Leo interrupted, laughing. "The mortgages are an investment that I mean to repay, and the painting a wedding gift. I was referring to your daughter. She is a gift beyond price. I believe I could not have a better mistress for Farthingale."

Momentarily nonplussed, Oliver said nothing more, but he was inordinately pleased. He stared at his daughter as she came back into the room. "I will say this, my lord, in truth, I have never seen Gillian in better looks."

Leo agreed, and kept private his concern that although his wife might appear well, she lacked her usual energy. For the past few weeks, she was inclined to retire early and sleep late. He had even caught her yawning at the theater during a performance of *Twelfth Night*, which she adored. He also knew she was still occasionally troubled by stomach pains and scolded her for her failure to see Dr. Westcot, which she promised him she would do when they returned home. Still, she insisted she felt well enough, and it was only the crowds and the constant rushing about that tired her.

They did have a press of social engagements; calls must be paid, for not to do so would be an unforgivable slight. They both agreed, however, that they would be well pleased to return to Farthingale. On Wednesday afternoon, Leo escorted his wife to Lady Tyndale's with nothing more pressing on his mind than his hope of meeting Sir Harry, who had been absent from Town, visiting a distant relative near Bath. Diana Beauclerk was also reportedly out of Town, so he was taken by surprise when she walked into the salon on the arm of Lord Fenwick.

His first thought was that she was even more beautiful than he'd recalled. She was pale, but that only enhanced her delicate complexion and made her green eyes appear larger than usual. He prayed she would not faint again.

But Miss Beauclerk had her emotions in hand. Her mother had warned her that Wrexham would likely be present and that she must greet him with a degree of composure. Diana could still hear her mother's voice, admonishing, "It was quite understandable that you swooned the last time you met, but if you do so again, the sympathy of the ton will accrue to Lady Wrexham. And you must think of Fenwick, too. Do not believe he will make you an offer if 'tis rumored about Town that you are still enamored of another. He may be taken with you, my dear, but he has his pride."

Diana knew her mother spoke the truth, and she had steeled herself to meet Leo. 'Twas not as difficult as her mother imagined. Lord Fenwick's steadfast attention had done much to soothe her wounded feelings over what she perceived as Wrexham's defection. There were even days that she did not think of Leo at all, and when she did, she consoled herself with the knowledge that Fenwick was not only considered the more handsome of the two but his title was of more consequence than Leo's— and there was no comparing their wealth. Of course, she also was cognizant that it was a feather in her cap to have him dancing attendance on her. Other misses had tried to ensnare him without success.

So when she saw Leo walk into the salon, the little American by his side, Diana lifted her chin, forced a smile to her lips, and murmured, "Lord Wrexham, how delightful to see you again. Will you not present me to your wife?"

The introductions were performed, and Lord Fenwick, having a very good idea of what Lady Wrexham must be feeling, offered her his arm and a compassionate smile. "I understand you are from Virginia. Perhaps you would do me the honor of taking a turn about the room with me? I confess, I would like to hear more about your country."

Leo watched them walk away with mixed feelings. He was thankful for an opportunity to speak to Diana privately, but it was rather like having a tempting dish set before one, and then being told not to touch it. One look at her pale beauty renewed all the feelings he thought he had set aside forever. But he was also conscious of his wife walking down the room with Fenwick. He would not for the world do ought that would embarrass or hurt her.

Diana's laughter, brittle and derisive, mocked him. "La, my lord, how provincial you have become! The way your eyes follow your wife clearly speaks of a gentleman in love."

He knew it was jealousy that made her speak so and replied softly, "We have come to terms with our arrangement. Gillian is very good to me, perhaps more than I deserve."

"Marriage with you apparently agrees with her," Diana replied tartly, her eyes on Lady Wrexham as she laughed at something Fenwick said. "She looks very well."

"Do you think so?" he asked, unaware of the concern in his voice.

Diana snapped her fan shut. "Obviously. I suppose she has not much sensibility. Tell me, my lord, do you remain in Town long?"

"Only a few more days. You *will* think me provincial,

but I am eager to return to Farthingale. There is so much work to be done—"

"Perhaps I shall see you there," she interrupted, toying with her fan. "I am going home myself. Mama has invited several guests to stay . . . Lord Fenwick is coming, and, oh, several of my particular friends. It shall be quite a gay party. Mayhap we will ride over to visit Farthingale and see your renovations. That is, of course, if you would not find such a visit intrusive?"

"Farthingale would be honored."

"Then perchance we shall call. I should like to see what . . . Lady Wrexham has done to the house. I do hope she has not made too many changes? You will think it foolish of me, but I have always loved it so, I would loathe to think of it made all new and refurbished. It would lose that splendid melancholy air I find so charming."

He smiled wryly. "If you mean by that the leaking roofs and smoking chimneys, they have been repaired. Other than badly needed repairs, the house itself is little changed, though I suppose it is more polished and better ordered. Gillian is an excellent housekeeper."

"Ah, Lady Wrexham," Diana said as she saw Gillian and Lord Fenwick drawing near. "I was just telling your husband that we shall be neighbors soon, and I hope to have the pleasure of calling on you."

"We would be most pleased," Gillian replied courteously, but her attention was on Leo. He did not appear distressed by his interlude with Miss Beauclerk, but he had been standing for some time, and she feared his leg might be paining him. She said nothing, however. She would not give Miss Beauclerk cause to think Leo lived under the cat's paw.

The conversation turned to hunting, for Farthingale was situated in Cotswold country. Gillian listened while the other three recalled past hunts. Or half listened.

165

Her thoughts wandered, her legs felt unusually heavy, and she longed to find a quiet place where she might sit down and close her eyes. Unfortunately, they still had two more calls to make before returning to their hotel.

She was deeply thankful a few moments later when Leo said they must take their leave. She murmured something appropriate, was grateful for the support of her husband's arm, and allowed him to lead her through the crowded salon. Her head had started to ache, and she felt a trifle dizzy. They were detained twice on the way out by friends of Leo's, but both conversations were mercifully brief.

Then she felt the cool air on her cheeks as they stepped outside, and after being helped into the carriage, sank tiredly into its cushioned seats.

"My dear, forgive me for saying so, but you look utterly exhausted. Shall we consign Lady Jersey to the devil and return to the hotel?"

"There is nothing I should like better," she replied with a wistful smile. "But it would only mean postponing the visit, and the next several days are already so full. . . ."

Her voice trailed off, and she leaned her head back against the squabs. Leo allowed her to rest until their carriage stopped before Lady Jersey's. Even then, he was reluctant to disturb her, but apparently the cessation of movement made her realize they had arrived. Her eyes fluttered open, and she said, "Oh, are we here so soon?"

"Yes, my dear, but are you certain you wish to go in?"

Gillian stirred herself. 'Twas ridiculous becoming so fatigued over a few house calls when she used to spend the day riding for hours, then presiding over dinner and dancing until dawn. Perhaps it was the climate, she thought. Leo had put down the steps and lifted his hand to assist her down.

She glanced down, and the ground beneath her spun dizzily. Her foot slipped, and she pitched forward into her husband's arms as a cloak of blackness settled around her.

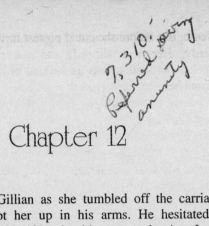

Chapter 12

Leo caught Gillian as she tumbled off the carriage steps and swept her up in his arms. He hesitated a moment, wondering if he should not carry her into Lady Jersey's and send immediately for a doctor. But he knew if he did so, the gossips would spread the tale all over Town, and heaven only knew what conjectures they would draw. He shifted her weight and managed to climb back into the landau, then ordered his groom to drive as quickly as possible to Grillon's Hotel.

He held Gillian in his arms, protecting her as much as he could from the bumps and sway of the carriage as it rolled across the cobblestones. She was so tiny, so fragile. He gazed down at the sprinkle of freckles across her nose and silently prayed no harm would come to her.

Gillian's lashes fluttered open. For a dazed moment, she stared up at him, uncertain what had happened. Then she struggled to sit up.

"Lie still, my dear," Leo ordered, firmly but gently. "You fainted, and I am taking you back to the hotel—and I want no arguments from you. We shall have the doctor in and discover what's amiss."

"But Lady Jersey," Gillian protested in a faint voice. In truth, she felt disinclined to move from the welcoming comfort of Leo's arms. She was so tired of the bustle and noise of London, so tired of paying calls, so tired of always being careful not to say or do anything to cause offense. But before she could protest further, the carriage rolled to a stop.

Postboys came running to assist Lord Wrexham as he descended from the landau with his wife in his arms. Oblivious to the gawking stares of strangers, he strode toward the hotel.

"Leo, this is ridiculous," Gillian said, blushing furiously as she met the astonished gaze of other guests. The skirt of her dress was wrapped tightly about her legs, and she could feel the cool air on her exposed ankles. Mortified, she appealed to him, "Pray, set me down. I am much better and quite capable of walking. Indeed, I cannot think how I came to faint, because I have never done so before."

He ignored her, carrying her through the entrance of the hotel and up the wide curving staircase to their suite of rooms. One of the hotel lads scurried ahead, and the door was opened by Thurston a few seconds before Leo reached it. He shouldered his way in and bore his wife straight through to their chamber, then deposited her on the bed.

"My lord," Thurston uttered, staring. "Did an accident befall Lady Wrexham? Is there ought I can do?"

"She swooned," he answered briefly as he stripped off his gloves and cape. He handed them to his valet. "Fetch a doctor here at once."

As Thurston hurried out, Lucy rushed in. "Oh, my lady, whatever happened?"

"Nothing to be alarmed about," Gillian replied as she tried to rise.

"You, madam, will stay put until the doctor has examined you," Leo told her, his hands gently forcing her to lie back on the bed.

"Leopold," Lady Barrows intoned from the door, "perhaps you will be so good as to explain why you felt it necessary to carry your wife through the street quite as though she were a member of the *demi monde*?"

Gillian, her face a bright red, closed her eyes and sank against the pillows. Leo released his wife's hands and glanced up at his aunt. "I don't know how you came to be here, ma'am, but I am most thankful to see you. We were about to pay a call on Lady Jersey when Gillian fainted. I have sent for the doctor, naturally, but—"

"My carriage arrived at Lady Jersey's just as you were leaving," Lady Barrows interrupted, her eyes on Gillian. "Naturally, I followed you, but there is no cause for this unseemly display."

"I fear you do not understand, ma'am. My wife has been unusually tired of late. She has complained of stomach pains, and now she has swooned. I believe I have every cause to be anxious."

"Really, Leopold, one would think with all your experience you would recognize the signs of a lady breeding."

Gillian's eyes flew open, and she stared at Lady Barrows in astonishment. She was no less amazed than her husband, who looked down at his wife and then back at his aunt. "You mean she . . . she is with child?"

Lady Barrows laughed, though not unkindly. "I suspect as much. It is rather a normal occurrence between a husband and a wife. Surely it cannot be entirely unexpected?"

Dazed, Leo reached for Gillian's hand. "I had not thought . . . we have been wed so short a time. . . ."

"It takes very little time to create a child," his aunt replied tartly. "Now, please leave us alone, Leopold. I wish to speak to your wife privately. If you desire to be of use, order her a cup of hot tea and some dry toast. You may send the doctor in when he arrives, but I have little doubt he will do anything but confirm my diagnosis."

Her nephew obeyed her. Still awed, he headed for the door.

"Leo?" Lady Barrows called. When he looked back, she smiled at him. "Congratulations, dear boy." Then she shooed Lucy from the room, propped two pillows behind Gillian's back, and suggested she would be more comfortable if she removed her hat and gloves.

Gillian obeyed her as one in a daze. She could think only of the child. Wishing to hear the words again, she said, "Are you quite sure that is why I fainted?"

"Trust me, dear, with three children of my own, not to mention numerous nieces and nephews, I believe I am sufficiently experienced to judge. I rather thought such might be the case when your presentation gown had to be altered. Do you want advice?"

Shyly Gillian nodded.

"Then return to Farthingale as soon as possible, and keep yourself busy. The more active you are while carrying the child, the easier the birth will be. Do not allow my nephew, your father, or any fool of a doctor to persuade you otherwise. You are a fine, healthy girl, and I see no reason why you should not bear a child with very little trouble."

"It was certainly easy enough to . . ." Too embarrassed to complete her thoughts, Gillian blushed again.

"Yes, well, we shall not discuss that," Lady Barrows said, looking down her long thin nose, but her eyes held a glimmer of amusement. "I shall leave you now, but remember what I have said, and if, when your time draws near, you would feel more comfortable with my presence, you may have Leopold send for me. Lavinia, I can tell you, will not be of the slightest use, though she will dote on the child once 'tis born. She always does so."

Lady Barrows left Gillian to consider this new and rather astonishing turn of affairs. She was still lying on the bed, her hand resting on her stomach, trying to imagine the child within, when Lucy returned to the room carrying a tray with tea and toast.

She placed it within easy reach, then asked, "Oh, miss, do you think Lady Barrows is right about the baby?"

Gillian nodded happily. She did not need the doctor's confirmation. Somehow, she had known the instant Leo's aunt had spoken that she was indeed with child. "I can scarce believe it, but I know 'tis true."

Lucy, her eyes admiring, said with a touch of awe, "It is just what you planned, ain't it, my lady? Marry his lordship, give him his heir, and then you're free to go back to Willowglen. I know how pleased you must be."

Gillian, feeling unaccountably depressed by the thought, agreed. It was what she had planned, but somehow Willowglen seemed so far away. Odd how quickly she had come to think of Farthingale as her home. Still, a bargain was a bargain, and she had told Leo she would leave after providing him an heir. She suspected he would be glad, though of course he was too much the gentleman to say so. But she had seen the way he looked at Miss Beauclerk this afternoon. One would have to be blind not to realize how much he still cared for that young lady. Sudden tears sprang to her eyes.

"My lady, what is it? Are you in pain?" Lucy asked.

"No," she declaimed, blinking back the tears. "I suppose 'tis just the shock of finding I am enceinte. My emotions are at sixes and sevens."

Her maid nodded knowingly. "I've heard ladies who are in the family way are given to sudden fits—happy as a lark one minute, then down in the mopes the next. You just drink your tea, and I expect you'll be feeling right as rain in no time. Think of your pa, my lady. I wonder what he will say when he learns he is to be a grandfather."

"Papa! Good heavens. Lucy, run and tell his lordship I must have a word with him. Oh, hurry, please."

She fretted for the few minutes it took before Leo stepped into the room. "What is it, my dear?" he asked as he came around the bed and sat down beside her. "I cannot think what is keeping that doctor."

"Leo," she said impatiently, "promise me you will not mention to Papa a word about the baby."

"Calm yourself, Gillian. I am certain it cannot be good for you or the child to disturb yourself in this manner. As for your father—why, of course he must be told, but I am sure he will be delighted."

"You do not understand," she cried, clutching at his hand. "Papa is—he will drive me mad. He cannot bear it when I am the least ill. After Mama died, he lost all faith in doctors. He will want me to stay in bed and cosset myself. Leo, you must not tell him! Promise me you will not."

He leaned down and kissed her brow. "My dear, do try to remain calm. I understand how you must feel, but we cannot keep such an event from him—it would be unconscionable, and your father would never forgive us."

"You will be sorry," she warned, her chin set mulishly.

He laughed and brought her hand up to his lips, kissing her fingers lightly. "How long do you think you can keep such a secret? In another month or two, he will know the truth merely by looking at you. Or do you mean to fob him off with an excuse that you have grown prodigiously fat? Ah, yes, I see how it may be done. Then, when my son is born, we shall say nothing. Having duped your father for nine months, we could not possibly own the truth. We will swear the servants to silence, and if your father comes to visit, we can pack the lad off to stay with my mother. He need never know."

She snatched her hand back. "You may choose to laugh at me, but tell Papa that I am with child and you will greatly regret it."

"At the moment, I am too well pleased to allow anything your father might say to overset me, but let us compromise. If the doctor is agreeable, then I suggest we remove at once to Farthingale. In a month or so, when you feel more able to cope, we shall invite your father and my mother for a visit. We can tell them our good news then."

It was not what she wished, but any delay found favor in her eyes. She nodded, then said pensively, "You do think it is good news?"

"The answer to my prayers," he assured her. "I will wait most impatiently for our child to be born."

The answer to his prayers. Was her husband remembering her own foolish promise and already anticipating the day when he would have Farthingale to himself again? Gillian might have questioned him further, but Thurston tapped on the door. "Dr. Knightsbridge is here, my lady."

They removed to Farthingale three days later. Gillian dealt with her future by simply not thinking of it. She told Lucy there would be time enough after the child was born to lay plans. And, after all, the babe might be a girl. She had questioned Leo extensively and knew that if he were to die without issue, his title, house, and lands would pass to the nearest male relative. A daughter could not inherit Farthingale.

Although no announcement was made directly to the servants, the word spread quickly that their mistress was with child—and nothing could have done more to endear Gillian to the staff than that welcome news. They rushed to do her bidding, watched her progress with eager eyes, and discussed her every ache and pain in the servants' hall. They wagered on whether her child would be a boy or girl and if the delivery would be difficult or easy.

Gillian, blissfully unaware of these discussions, altered her routine only slightly. Now that she knew the cause of her queasiness in the mornings and the reason for her sudden bouts of fatigue in the late afternoons, she planned her day accordingly. She slept later than was her custom, partook only of dry toast and tea on first rising, and rested in the afternoon. Leo might have worried over the little she ate for breakfast did she not come to dinner with a ravenous appetite and look so very well.

Pregnancy agreed with Gillian. Her blue eyes glowed brilliantly, and her hair seemed to have more luster. There was an air of assurance about her that had been previously lacking, and conversely, her manner toward the servants had softened. She no longer spoke sharply, and her natural impatience to have all set right at once was curbed.

Leo remarked on it one evening when they were sitting in the library after dinner. He had been going over his accounts, while she sat nearby with her sewing. He put aside his books, watching her for a moment, then rose and crossed around the desk. He dropped a light kiss on her brow.

Surprised, Gillian looked up. "You appear inordinately smug, my lord, rather like a fox in the henhouse."

"I have reason," he said, taking the chair next to her and stretching out his long legs. "My wife is looking exceptionally lovely, the household is running more efficiently than it has ever done, and the accounts are in excellent order. I believe I may begin to start repaying your father next year."

She bent her head over her sewing. It was useless to tell Leo he need not repay the mortgages; he was determined to do so. She supposed that if theirs had been a regular marriage, he might not have felt so obliged, but he hated being indebted to her father.

When she said nothing, he asked, "What is that you are working on, my dear? Something for the baby?"

"A christening gown," she replied, and held it up for his approval. Made of the finest white linen, delicate lace lined the collar and sleeves, and she had worked a pale pink ribbon in an intricate pattern down the front.

"Very pretty," he said, "but I hope you are making two. I should not like to see my son swaddled in such a feminine dress."

"Are you so certain the child will be a boy?"

"I am. 'Tis a Wrexham tradition. The firstborn is always a son, which puts me in mind that we must choose a name. Would you object if we were to name him after my father and yours? Augustus Oliver Reed . . . sounds impressive, do you not agree?"

"Very," she said softly as she bent her head once more over her stitches. "Papa will be very gratified."

"And you, Gillian?"

"I still believe you are rushing your fences. The child may very well be a girl. I suggest we wait until we are sure before choosing names."

"We could always call her Augusta Olivia," he teased.

"I would prefer Leonie," Gillian replied. *She should have something to remind her of her father.* The thought went unspoken, but it brought quick tears to her eyes. Heavens, she was becoming a regular watering pot. Blinking back the tears, she ducked her head so Leo would not see and hastily started to gather up her sewing.

"Are you leaving me?" Leo asked.

Forever, she thought, but she could not say that. Aloud, she murmured, "I am rather tired. If you will forgive me, I believe I shall retire."

"Allow me to carry that for you," he replied, rising as he spoke to reach for her sewing basket.

"Pray, do not disturb yourself. I can manage quite easily."

"Perhaps, but you must permit me to be of some use. It seems rather unfair that you should bear the burden of carrying our child while I am little more than an interested observer."

She managed a credible smile. "I would not say so, my lord. If I recollect, it was your rather active participation that resulted in my present condition."

He slipped an arm about her waist. His voice was soft against her hair. "I do not seem to remember. Perhaps if you were to demonstrate . . ."

The days slipped away, July sliding into August, with nothing occurring to mar the tranquillity of Farthingale until the afternoon when Diana Beauclerk called. Leo was with his agent on one of the farms, and Gillian had just decided to rest when Partridge came to inform her that callers had arrived. For a brief moment she was tempted to deny herself, but she knew she must not. She sighed, then instructed Partridge to show her guests to the rose drawing room and inform them she would be down directly.

Gillian ran a comb through her hair and decided against changing her morning dress. No matter what she wore, she could not hope to compete with Miss Beauclerk. Entering the drawing room a few moments later, Gillian warmly welcomed her visitors.

"I know it is frightfully rude of me to call in this manner," Miss Beauclerk said with one of her airy laughs, "but we were out riding, and when I mentioned we were near to Farthingale, Miss Sinclair simply insisted that we stop. Oh, may I make you known to my brother? And I believe you are acquainted with Lord Fenwick?"

Gillian acknowledged the gentlemen and smiled at Miss Sinclair, who looked rather astonished at learning she was the reason for the visit. "Pray, do not apologize. We receive so few visitors, I am certain Leo will be delighted. Unfortunately, he is occupied on one of the

177

farms this morning, but I shall send word to him, and I expect that by the time we have all had a cup of tea, he will be here. Sit down, do."

It was an ill-at-ease party, save for Fenwick, who appeared much amused. Gillian lacked the knack of conversing politely with people for whom she had no real liking, but she made the effort for her husband's sake. Tea was brought in by Minna, and Cook, on learning of the guests, sent in a tray of cookies and small cakes, which did the house proud.

"Gracious, how prosperous everything looks," Diana remarked when the maid, crisp and efficient in her new uniform, had left. "I vow I scarce know the place, though I must have had tea in this room a dozen times."

"Do you find it much changed?" Gillian, who had not dared move so much as a chair, asked. "I assure you, I have taken pains not to alter anything. The curtains and chair covers are new, of course, but they are identical to the original patterns."

"Oh, 'tis lovely, a vast improvement, I am sure," Diana replied, her gaze traveling about the room. The drawing room had always been comfortable in a scruffy sort of way. It was still comfortable, of course, but now it had the air of a well-tended house. The windows sparkled, the tops of the tables gleamed, and she was willing to wager a gloved finger run along the top of the mantel would not reveal so much as a speck of dust. She smiled at her hostess. "I am being foolishly sentimental, I know, to feel such attachment for the past, but I do hate to see this dear old place made all new and shining."

As no one else in the party had ever visited Farthingale, they could not comment on the room, and an awkward pause ensued. Lord Fenwick broke the silence saying, "Whatever changes have occurred, 'tis clear they agree with you, Lady Wrexham. I must say you appear in exceptional health. I fancy we may expect to hear an interesting announcement soon."

Gillian blushed as Fenwick's knowing eyes raked over her figure. There was no mistaking his meaning, but she had not thought her condition so readily apparent.

"La, Vitalis, what sort of announcement?" Diana demanded.

Gillian said hurriedly, "Perhaps he is referring to the new breed of sheep my husband has been experimenting with. He is crossing the Cotswold with, I believe, an Oxford. If he is successful, he tells me it will double the amount of wool they produce."

"Breeding is always a fascinating topic," Fenwick replied, a devilish glint of amusement in his eyes.

"Well, I do not think it a proper subject for the drawing room," Diana stated. "And, I own, I am astonished that Lord Wrexham would interest himself in such matters. When we used to walk in the ruins here, we talked of the glorious history of the house, of the spirits of the past whose presence one can still sense in certain spots, of the poetry that is the essence of Farthingale."

Philip Beauclerk looked with disgust at his sister. He had been against calling on Wrexham, but Fenwick had not objected, and, of course, Miss Sinclair would do whatever Diana wished, so he had gone along with the plan. But this romanticizing of Farthingale, of Wrexham, was going too far. If his sister was not careful, she would lose Fenwick, an alliance that neither she nor the family could afford to whistle down the wind. Aloud, he said, "Odd, my recollections are very different. Seems to me Wrexham was always eager to make improvements here. I recall him speaking to his father about it several times, but the old earl was too preoccupied with the Regent's set to waste his blunt on the house or land."

"For my part, I think it a very pretty house," Miss Sinclair ventured.

A quarter hour passed with awkward starts and stops in the conversation, so that when Leo appeared, he was greeted with a great deal of relief. He had been informed by Gillian's note that Miss Beauclerk was among the guests, so he affected no surprise and greeted her much as he would any old friend. He drew Miss Sinclair into the conversation, spoke to Philip about their adjoining properties, and to Fenwick about the latest gossip in Town. In a very short time, he had set his guests at ease.

Gillian, closely observing her husband, said little. She saw the way his eyes were involuntarily drawn to Miss Beauclerk, the pleasure that lurked there as he drank in her delicate beauty. He could not be blamed. The lady was attired in a pale blue riding habit, sleek and well fitted to her slender figure, a far cry from Gillian's own loosely fitted day dress, which had to be altered to accommodate the weight that she had gained.

"I was hoping we might have a tour of the ruins," Miss Beauclerk was saying. She referred to the foundation and crumpled walls of an old church beyond the formal gardens. "Imagine, Miss Sinclair, walking the same paths that monks might have trod five hundred years ago. If one is very still and very quiet, one can almost feel their presence."

Miss Sinclair shivered. "Heavens, is it haunted?"

"Oh, no, not haunted in the sense you mean. I believe the spirits of the monks do linger there, but 'tis a benign presence, as though they watch over all who enter."

"What balderdash," Philip interrupted. "I spent as much time in those gardens as you did, and the only thing I ever felt was the unyielding face of a boulder I tripped over chasing John."

Diana ignored him and turned with a poignant look to Wrexham. "Leo, you understand what I mean, do you not? How well I remember walking there with you in the late afternoon, the sun streaking over the hills and gilding all it touched."

Leo neither agreed nor disagreed, but he laughed, dispelling the mood. "I pray you will not set it about that there are ghosts on the grounds—the servants would desert us en masse—but 'tis a lovely walk in the afternoon. If you would like to see it again?"

"I should not wish to put you to any trouble, my lord," Diana replied demurely.

"Well, I certainly would enjoy seeing it," Miss Sinclair said. "Miss Beauclerk has spoken so rapturously about the place, I quite believe it must be the loveliest walk in all England."

"Then I hope you will not be disappointed," Leo replied, rising. "I fear memory sometimes has a way of playing us false. Sadly, things are seldom as perfect as one recollects."

"I am inclined to agree with you, my lord, but let us all go and look at your ruins, else Diana will not be satisfied," Philip said as he came to his feet, then bowed to Miss Sinclair, offering her his arm.

Gillian declined to join the others, saying she had already seen the ruins, and done sufficient walking for one day. She would remain at the house and arrange for cooling drinks for their guests on their return. Leo glanced at his wife, his eyes questioning her silently. She answered him with a shake of her head and a small smile. "Do go with your friends, Leo. I shall be quite content to remain here."

Lord Fenwick bowed to her. "If you will permit, Lady Wrexham, I shall stay and bear you company. I have seen enough ruins to last a lifetime."

She was surprised by his offer but agreed to it, and with creditable composure saw her husband walk off with Miss Beauclerk on his arm, followed by the lady's brother and

Miss Sinclair. Aware of Fenwick's appraising gaze, Gillian fussed with the teapot. "More tea, my lord?"

He declined as courteously as he had the walk in the gardens, then stretched out his long legs and gazed appreciatively at her. "That was well done of you, Lady Wrexham . . . allowing your husband to escort Miss Beauclerk. I am almost certain she had not anticipated such good fortune."

"To see the ruins? How could we refuse, sir, when she had ridden such a long way? It would have been unkind to have disappointed her."

Fenwick chuckled. "I cannot decide if you are terribly naive or more cleverly sophisticated than I had assumed. Tell me, my dear, are you not the tiniest bit concerned that Wrexham is at this moment strolling in a secluded area accompanied by a young lady with whom he is rumored to be deeply enamored?"

Gillian sat her cup down, folded her hands in her lap, and looked at him directly. "Apparently you are an advocate of plain speaking, my lord, so let me say frankly that I will not discuss my husband with you or anyone else."

"Have I offended you, my dear?" he asked with a lazy smile. "You must believe that it was not my intention. On the contrary, I had rather hoped that we might be friends, particularly since we have so much in common. You see, I intend to make Miss Beauclerk my wife."

"I congratulate you, Lord Fenwick, but I fail to see how that concerns me."

"No? It is perhaps gauche of me, but I prefer that my bride not be languishing after a gentleman with whom she once fancied herself in love. I say fancied, my lady, because I am certain it was little more than a young girl's romantic infatuation. Given the normal course of events, I doubt anything would have come of it."

"They were practically betrothed," Gillian protested.

"No, my dear. Oh, they had perhaps pledged their love

as young people tend to do, but there was no formal arrangement, and I doubt there would have been. Unfortunately, your husband's reversal of fortune, his need to marry an heiress, invested the situation with a romantic tragedy certain to appeal to one of Miss Beauclerk's sentimental nature."

"You are a cynic, sir."

"Merely practical," he replied. "Come, my lady, if you are honest you will admit there was never a more ill-suited pair. My Diana requires a gentleman of romantic turn who will indulge her flights of fancy and quote poetry to her. Your husband is more concerned with the success of his sheep-breeding experiments and restoring his estates. Given time, they would have driven each other mad."

Gillian picked up her cup and sipped it as she considered his words. She would like to have believed him, but there was a flaw. "You are most persuasive, my lord, but I understand Leo and Miss Beauclerk have known each other all their lives. They played together here as children."

"And then he joined the military and went away. He returned home wounded, a most romantic hero—of course Diana immediately fancied herself in love. But I doubt they spent above a dozen hours together. We must remedy that, Lady Wrexham, for both our sakes. I propose we allow them a great deal of time together . . . time to realize how ill suited they are. You might start by inviting us to dinner one evening."

Chapter 13

Gillian was not entirely sure Lord Fenwick's theory was correct, but the Beauclerks and their guests were invited to return to Farthingale for dinner on the following Friday. Leo appeared surprised when she extended the invitation, but he did not seem to anticipate the event or be unduly disturbed by it. The dinner, in Gillian's opinion, turned out to be a tedious affair. Miss Beauclerk had little conversation. She was interested in the latest fashions, gossip, and poetry. She read little and confided she thought Lord Byron wonderfully romantic. But, however lacking she might be as a conversationalist, there could be no denying that she was beautiful, and she had a fragile air of helplessness that made the gentlemen rush to her assistance. Leo included.

It was a mistake, Gillian thought, to have the woman in the house—a constant reminder to Leo of what might have been. And afterward, in the drawing room, Miss Beauclerk sat at the newly tuned spinet playing skillfully and singing in her soft, low voice. She chose a ballad about unrequited love and looked directly at Leo as she sang.

Gillian covertly watched her husband. Impossible to tell what he thought. He sat quietly beside her, an attentive look on his face, and seemed immersed in the music. When Miss Beauclerk was done, he was lavish in his praise, remarking that he could not recall when he had enjoyed a performance so much. Gillian, who did not sing at all and played competently but without Miss Beauclerk's flair, felt hugely inadequate.

Huge, she told herself, was the right adjective. She was achingly aware of how much weight she had gained. She could never aspire to Miss Beauclerk's classical beauty, of course, but standing next to the tall blond emphasized her own short and now-rotund figure. Desolate, her back aching and her head beginning to throb, she willed the evening to end, but it was another hour before Leo showed their guests out.

He returned to find his wife ensconced in a wing chair drawn near the fire, her feet elevated on a stool, her head back, and her eyes closed. He drew up the chair opposite and said, "Poor darling, are you very tired? I asked Minna to bring you a cup of hot chocolate."

"Thank you," she replied, opening her eyes to meet his concerned gaze. She immediately felt guilty and smiled at him. "Do not fret. 'Tis merely that I have not the energy I once did."

"All the same, promise that you will have breakfast in bed tomorrow and rest a little."

She said nothing as Minna entered with a cup of chocolate for her and a glass of wine for Leo. When the maid left, she cradled the cup in her hands, liking the warmth of it, and idly watched the fire.

"I fear we have become rather spoiled," Leo said. At her inquisitive glance, he added with a rueful smile, "Entertaining visitors is all very well, but I confess it seemed to me that our guests would never leave. I was worried about you, too. Is your back paining you?"

"Not very," she replied, then tentatively, "Miss Beauclerk played the spinet beautifully, I thought."

He looked embarrassed. "Do you suppose she realized I was not paying attention? I could not help thinking about the experiments we're conducting, which reminds

185

me, I must see Halthorpe tomorrow. If we can scrape together enough money, there are three rams I want to buy. They are from Dorchester's herd, and he is willing to sell them in exchange for part of the new breed—if we're successful."

Immeasurably pleased to know that it was the farm he'd been thinking of and warmed that she was his confidante at the end of the day, Gillian listened contentedly as her husband discussed his plans. If it was new rams he wanted, then rams he should have. She suggested, "Leo, Papa would advance you the money you need, and be happy to do so."

"I know," he said, reaching across for her hand. "I hope you don't think I am foolish, but this is something I would do without his assistance. But speaking of your father, I think that it is time we—"

"Oh, good heavens!" she interrupted, a strange look on her face. "Leo, the baby moved!"

He rose at once and came to her side, kneeling by the chair. She placed his hand on her stomach. "There! Do you feel it?"

"My son," he murmured, awed, as he felt the flutter of movement beneath his fingers.

"Or your daughter," she reminded him.

"Augustus Oliver," he teased as he stood up, but he leaned over and kissed her affectionately, then lightly brushed her cheek with his fingers. "I believe this occasion calls for something stronger than wine."

He crossed the room to the cabinet where various liquors were stored, and poured himself a generous portion of brandy. As he returned to his chair, he told her, "You realize, of course, that this settles the matter. Our respected parents must be informed at once. If you will write to your father, I will write my mother."

She sighed as she agreed, knowing the visit could not be put off any longer. Her father would be hurt that she had kept the news from him for this long. And how could she explain that she was cherishing these days alone with Leo? Aloud, she said, "Do you think it would be best to have them here at separate times? Perhaps your mother for a fortnight, then my father?"

"Impossible. Your father would feel slighted if we told Mother first, and she would never forgive us if he learned of the news before her. No, my dear, they must be told together and as soon as possible, but consider the advantages. We extend one invitation for a fortnight, then we shall soon be alone again. If we asked them to visit on separate occasions, it would mean having guests for the next month."

She smiled at his reasoning, conceding he was right. The letters were duly posted the next day, and replies received within the week. The dowager, as might be expected, wrote that she could ill afford the post charges, complained living in Bath was shockingly dear, and Clarissa the least sympathetic of all her children. She greatly missed her dear Leo and would somehow contrive to cover the expenses of the journey if her son had need of her.

Oliver Prescott replied in his frank way that it was high time his little girl remembered him, and they could expect him on the twenty-fourth, and added a postscript that if there was anything Gillian desired from Town, she must let him know.

"We ought to suggest something," Gillian said, after reading the letter aloud to Leo during breakfast. "He will feel constrained to bring us some sort of gift, you know."

"Egad, do you mean like a pair of peacocks? My dear, pray tell him I would much appreciate a bottle or two of that excellent Bordeaux he served me. Will that suffice, do you think?"

Gillian wrinkled her nose. "He will probably think it mere trumpery, but we shall see. I shall write to him this

187

afternoon." She did so, telling him that Leo would appreciate a bottle or two of wine, but begged her father not to bring anything else as the dowager was coming also, and might feel embarrassed at arriving empty-handed. Gillian tactfully pointed out her mother-in-law's straitened circumstances and that even the post charges for the journey would be difficult for her to bear. Her letter brought results, but not quite the outcome she had anticipated.

On the twenty-fourth, Gillian nervously inspected the green bedchamber. She had no idea why it was called the green room, since nothing in it was green. The best of the guest rooms, it was decorated in soft shades of blue, with blue and gold silk hangings and a blue and cream love seat. Mrs. Sewell, when asked, replied only that they could not call it the blue room, could they, since the blue room was across the hall.

Whatever it was called, Gillian thought it looked very pretty and inviting. Fresh flowers stood on the center table near the love seat and on the secretary in front of the long windows. It was spotlessly clean, and a fire had been laid, ready to be lit the instant the dowager arrived. Not that it was cold. Gillian thought the day exceptionally warm, and in her own room had set the windows open to catch the breeze. But Leo had warned her that his mother chilled easily and had always complained of the draftiness of Farthingale.

She adjusted a curtain to hang more smoothly, placed a new novel on the bedside table, and was wondering if she should have a dish of fresh fruit brought up, when she heard the sound of carriage wheels. Hastily tidying her new dress, which a seamstress had specially cut to conceal the fullness of her stomach, Gillian hurried below stairs. She wanted to be in the hall to properly welcome the dowager, or her father, should he arrive first.

Partridge opened the door, and Gillian caught the sound of girlish laughter and Lady Clarissa's high voice. "Thank you again, Papa Prescott. He is the dearest thing."

The young girl entered the hall a second later, a spaniel pup cuddled in her arms. "Oh, Gillian—I may call you that now that we are sisters, may I not?—only look what your papa has given me! It is the dearest creature, and I hope you do not object that I brought him. Papa Prescott said you would not."

"No, Lady Clarissa, not at all," Gillian replied, not certain which question she was answering. She accepted her sister-in-law's kiss on the cheek, caressed the spaniel's silky ears, and asked, "But how did you come to be traveling with my father?"

"Surprised you, eh, puss?" Oliver boomed as he assisted the dowager into the hall. "As soon as I had your letter, I fired off one to my lady here and told her to leave all the arrangements to me. Nothing simpler than calling for her and Lady Clarissa on the way. In truth, it made for a most enjoyable journey—far better than if I had traveled up here on my own."

He enveloped his daughter in a bear hug as he spoke, then stepped back, beaming proudly at his surprise.

"That was . . . most kind of you, Papa." Her eyes flew to her mother-in-law. Lavinia appeared pale, and rather shaken. Gillian stepped forward, kissed her lightly on the cheek, and begged, "Do come in. Whatever Papa may say, I am sure you must be fatigued from so long a drive. Would you prefer to be shown to your room at once or to have a cup of tea first?"

"My room," the dowager murmured in failing accents. Her dark eyes surveyed the hall. "Where is Leopold?"

"He asked me to make his apologies if you arrived before he returned," Gillian explained as she linked her arm in her mother-in-law's and led her toward the steps.

"He had urgent business on one of the farms, but he will be home directly."

Lavinia's brows rose. "Indeed? I cannot conceive of what business could be so important he cannot be at home to welcome his mother, particularly when I have come at his request. But I suppose he is just like his father, with never a thought for anyone else."

"Oh, no, pray do not say so. He has taken such pains to see that everything possible has been provided for your comfort." At the top of the stairs, her mother-in-law started to the right, but Gillian gently guided her steps to the left. "We have put you in the blue guest room. I think it the nicest of all the bedchambers."

"How foolish of me . . . naturally I cannot expect to have my old room. For thirty years I slept in the west wing . . . but I suppose I shall adjust. I only hope the blue room does not get the morning sun."

"I am afraid it does, but I shall instruct the maid to draw the curtains so you will not be disturbed."

"Never mind, dear. Wilson, my dresser, will attend to it. She is following in the fourgon with the baggage. I do hope she remembered to pack my vinaigrette. I am feeling rather faint."

They stepped into the bedchamber, and Lavinia looked about with keen eyes, noting the new curtains, bed-covers, and cushions. She sighed. "I see you have refurbished the room. I hope it was not on my account. Young people are so quick to throw out the old. I suppose it is only when one is my age that one develops a sentimentality for reminders of the past."

There seemed to be nothing to say to that, and Gillian gestured toward the fireplace. "Would you like to have the fire lit?"

"In the middle of the day? My dear, I realize your father is prodigiously wealthy, but my son is not. You must learn to practice economies."

Below stairs, Leo had returned and was faring little better with his father-in-law. Oliver had expected a much larger and grander estate than Farthingale. Disappointment rife in his voice, he pronounced it "a tidy little house," but added despairingly, "Of course, I can see it's been let go, and I'll wager it is as cold as the devil in winter. You don't intend to remain here once the weather turns, do you, my boy?"

"Well, yes, rather, but 'tis not the hardship you imagine, sir. My family has lived here for generations. Indeed, both Clarissa and I grew up here, and you can see it has not harmed us in the least."

Oliver did not press the issue, but he was determined to get his daughter to remove before the first snowfall. If he was any judge, she'd be housebound once winter set in. Of course she weathered hard winters at Willowglen, but that house had been well built and furnished with every modern contrivance. This drafty barn of a place was very different. It might do well enough for his lordship, who was used to such conditions, but Gillian would likely take sick. The specter of his wife, who had died of pneumonia, still haunted him, and he would not risk his daughter dying of the same illness.

Fortunately, Clarissa came dancing into the room at that moment, her new puppy frisking at her heels. "Leo, how well you look! Gillian must be taking great care of you. And the house is so very pretty, much nicer than when Mama and I lived here."

"Thank you. I need not ask you how you are doing, for I can see you are in spirits. What of Mother? Is she much fatigued from the drive?"

Clarissa grinned. "To hear her, one would say so, but we traveled in the greatest style with *two* outriders and footmen to see to our comfort. Papa Prescott called for us, and look what he brought me, Leo. Is it not the darlingest puppy?"

Her brother, envisioning his mother enclosed in a post chaise with his father-in-law, Clarissa, and a lively spaniel for above six hours, felt a surge of unaccustomed sympathy for his mother. Hard put not to laugh, he turned to Oliver. "That was most kind of you, sir."

A footman stepped into the room. "Pardon me, my lord, but Sir Harry has called and wishes a word with you."

"Show him in," Leo replied, thinking it was high time his old friend returned home. He had spent an unconscionable time in Bath . . . then he caught the look of eager anticipation in his sister's eyes and noticed the way she quickly brushed an errant curl off her shoulder. So that was the way the wind was blowing.

Gillian suggested they wait until after dinner to announce their glad tidings, but Leo held that it would do much to placate their respective in-laws and provide a mutual topic of conversation for so ill assorted a dinner party. He stood at the head of the table, his mother seated on his left and his father-in-law on his right. Oliver had Clarissa seated next to him, and Sir Harry, who had not required much urging to remain, sat opposite her, next to the dowager. Gillian, nervously watching her husband, graced the foot of the table.

Leo had opened a bottle of the Bordeaux his father-in-law had brought as a gift, and ordered the footmen to fill the glasses. Now he lifted his own, the cut crystal sparkling in the candlelight. "I should like to make a toast, and I hope that you will join me. All of you were present five months ago when Miss Gillian Prescott did me the great honor of becoming my wife." He paused, looking at each of his guests in turn. Then, his gaze fixed on Gillian, he said quietly, "I give you Lady Wrexham. In the months past, her presence here has enriched this house beyond my greatest expectations. No gentleman could wish for a better wife, a better chatelaine . . . or a better mother for his children. Pray, join me in drinking to her health, and the well-being of the child she carries."

Astonished silence met his speech as it took a moment for the meaning of his words to penetrate, and then everyone spoke at once.

Oliver gazed at his daughter and said gruffly, "Well, I'll be! Here I thought you was just putting on a bit of weight. So I am to be a grandpa, eh?"

Lavinia's eyes lit with joy. "You deserve me not to speak to you for keeping such splendid news from me! The heir to Farthingale." Her eyes flew to Gillian. "My dear, dear daughter, you have given me a gift beyond price. Oh, there is so much we must discuss. Perhaps after dinner . . ."

Harry lifted his glass, grinned at his friend, and mouthed "Well done." Then he smiled at Gillian. "Pray accept my felicitations, Lady Wrexham. 'Tis wonderful news."

Clarissa said, "I do hope you have a boy, Gillian. I already have so many nieces. What shall you name the child?"

Gillian, blushing prettily as she received their best wishes, said in her soft drawl, "Leo is convinced our child will be a boy, in the true Wrexham tradition, and wishes to name him Augustus Oliver after both our fathers."

"Well, now, I'd not look for such a compliment," Oliver said, his eyes suspiciously bright. "Augustus Oliver Reed—it has a nice ring to it. I say, will the lad be an earl?"

"Not until I die," Leo replied, and laughed at his father-in-law's disappointment. "But pray do not look so crest-fallen, sir. Outside the family, your grandson will be addressed as 'my lord.' "

Beaming proudly, Oliver looked at his daughter. "If

only your mama, God rest her sweet soul, could have lived to see this moment. She would have been so proud. Now then, when can we expect this babe?"

"In January," Gillian replied, blushing anew at how quickly she had conceived.

"So soon!" Oliver said, and calculating rapidly, figured, "Why, that's less than five months, and dozens of arrangements yet to be made. When are you removing to London? And you'll not be staying at a hotel, my girl. I shall put my house at your disposal—or lease you one if you'd prefer that. Have to arrange for an accoucheur, too." He turned to the dowager. "My lady, you likely know—who's the best to be had in London?"

"Papa," Gillian said quietly. "We are not removing to London. I shall have the child here, and I have consulted Dr. Westcot several times. There is no reason for you to be concerned."

"An excellent man," Lavinia approved.

"Not move?" Oliver boomed. "Are you mad? You cannot mean to stay in this barn of a place! Why, suppose it snows and the doctor cannot reach you? I won't have it."

"Perhaps we could discuss this after dinner," Leo suggested. "In private."

"No, sir! I don't see that there is ought to discuss. I shall take Gillian back to London with me, and that's the end of it."

Leo sighed and set down his glass. Only the tiny pulse in his temple betrayed his anger. He signaled a footman, gave orders dinner was to be set back an hour, then glanced at his friend. "Harry?"

"By jove, I believe a walk before dinner would improve my appetite," his friend said obligingly, and pushed back his chair. "Lady Clarissa, would you join me in a turn about the gardens?"

Lavinia looked ready to do battle with Prescott, but Leo laid a hand on hers. "Mama, would you and Gillian please excuse us? I should like to speak to my father-in-law privately."

"Leo, I think I should stay," Gillian said, glancing apprehensively between him and her father.

Some of his temper abated as he looked at his wife and saw the worry in her eyes. "You need not be concerned, my dear. Your father and I will settle this between us . . . like gentlemen."

Lavinia rose and came around to Gillian's chair. "Perhaps it would be best, my dear, if we retired to the drawing room."

Leo waited until the ladies had left the room, then smiled at his father-in-law. "Can we not discuss this matter rationally, sir? I believe we both have Gillian's welfare at heart."

Oliver drained his glass and slammed it against the table. "I do, but I can't say as much for you—not if you mean to keep her here in the dead of winter, and her with child. I won't have it, I tell you."

"I am sorry to disillusion you, sir, but you have nothing to say in the matter."

"Nothing to say?" Oliver roared, and rose to his feet. Towering over Leo, he threatened, "It's my daughter we're talking about! You think you can keep her here against my will? Well, let me tell you, my fine lord, I'll call in the mortgages so fast your head will spin. You'll not have this place above a week."

Leo, the blood draining from his face, stood as well. Remembering his promise to Gillian, he tried to check his anger, but his voice was barely civil as he replied, "You must do as you think best, Mr. Prescott. But even if you foreclosed on the mortgages, Gillian and I would remain in the country. It may have escaped your notice, but she is much happier here than ever she was in Town. It was her choice to bear the child at Farthingale."

Oliver's jaw worked as he strove to find words.

Seldom had anyone ever had the gumption to stand up to him, and that it should be his son-in-law who had everything to lose, flabbergasted him. His hands clenched into fists, and he roared, "If she said that, it was only to please you. She knows you married her to save this pile of stones—'tis the house you care about, not her. But she's all I got, and I'll not see her die because she didn't have the best doctors to attend her."

Realizing a great deal of his father-in-law's bluster was due to fear, Leo replied quietly, "If that is what you think, you are much mistaken."

"Are you trying to gammon me you didn't marry her to save this wretched place? You'll catch cold at that. It was a marriage of convenience—plain and simple—and you'll not be convincing me else."

"I don't deny it, but our circumstances have altered. Come, sir, you have known her all her life—can you believe that anyone could live with Gillian for five months without realizing her true worth? I care very deeply for her. As for your wife, I sincerely regret you suffered such a misfortune, but the cases are very different. I assure you, I shall take the greatest care of Gillian."

Some of the rage left Oliver, for there could be no doubting the sincerity in his son-in-law's voice. But he was ill accustomed to not having his own way, and not yet ready to concede, said gruffly, "My lord, I am giving you fair warning—if anything happens to my girl, I shall hold you personally to blame."

"No more than I would myself," Leo answered gravely. He placed a hand on Oliver's shoulder. "Let us discuss this later when we are both calmer. Cook is no doubt agitated at having dinner set back—"

"Dinner! Do you think I would set down with you? You've enough brass to outfit a ship!"

"I was thinking of Gillian, sir. You must know it

would distress her to think we were on the outs." Knowing he held a trump card, Leo played it. "Dr. Westcot believes it important that she not be agitated. If we could sit down to dinner and behave civilly, it would do much to ease her mind."

"Oh, very well—have 'em in. But don't think you've heard the last of this, my lord. And I intend to see this doctor you're so keen on for myself."

"Thank you for staying," Leo said as he saw Sir Harry out later that evening. They stood on the front steps, waiting for Harry's gig to be brought up from the stables. The evening was cool and lit by a half moon against a field of glittering stars. It had been a long day, and he was tired, but he owed his friend a debt of gratitude and said, "Your presence probably prevented another family squabble."

"My pleasure, old fellow. Can't say it was the best dinner I've sat through, but it was far from the worst. Pity Lady Barrows wasn't here. She'd set your father-in-law straight quick enough."

"Lord, don't remind me. She's coming in December and will stay until the child is born. Oddly enough, my wife seems to like her. The pair of them were as thick as thieves before we left London. I've never seen my aunt take to anyone as she has to Gillian."

"Well, I'm not surprised. One can't help but like your wife. She's a charming girl."

"Yes, I've come to realize that. . . ."

When Leo said nothing more, Harry tapped him on the arm. "If you want a bit of advice, I suggest you tell her so. Unless I miss my guess, Gillian is under the impression that you are still pining for Diana."

"She can't be," Leo said, dismissing the idea out of hand. "Why, when Diana called here with Fenwick—

197

Gillian must have seen that I treated her with only the courtesy due an old friend."

"Which," Harry pointed out, grinning hugely, "is precisely how you would have behaved if you were still carrying a torch for her. Egad, Leo, can you really be so thickheaded? You formed a marriage of convenience. How is your wife to know that your feelings have undergone a change unless you tell her so?"

He could not believe it and shook his head. "No, you must be mistaken."

The sound of carriage wheels crunching on the graveled drive signaled one of the grooms was approaching with Harry's carriage. He tossed away his cigar, hesitated, then said, "Leo, there's something I think you should know. Your wife is planning to return to America once she presents you with an heir."

"That was her original plan, but she has not mentioned it in months."

"Maybe not to you, but the servants are talking about it. Her abigail let something slip to one of the kitchen maids. You know what the gossip mill is like. We heard about it at Rosewood—at least my mother did, and she questioned me."

"Gossip!" Leo retorted. "You should know better than to listen to such nonsense."

Harry shrugged and sauntered down the steps. He took the reins from the groom, then called back, "If I were you, I wouldn't take any chances. For once in your life, let down that stoic reserve of yours and tell the girl how you feel. Unless, of course, you don't care enough."

Chapter 14

By the time Leo returned to his guests, both Gillian and her father had retired. Clarissa had taken her pup out on the terrace, so only his mother remained in the drawing room. She, too, was ready for her bed, but she had waited to give her son a bit of advice.

Lavinia patted the cushion next to her on the sofa. "Come sit with me for a moment. There is something I particularly wish to say to you."

"Can it not wait until the morrow?" Leo asked. Harry's parting shot had troubled him more than he cared to admit. He wanted to talk to Gillian before she fell asleep.

"I shall not keep you above a moment or two," Lavinia promised, and tugged his hand until he sat beside her. "In many respects, you are like your father, and that can be very hard on a young wife like Gillian—particularly since she is not accustomed to our ways. A marriage of convenience . . ."

Leo sighed, only half listening. First his father-in-law, then his best friend, and now his mother lecturing him. He was tired of hearing about his marriage of convenience—a misnomer if ever he heard one. There was nothing the least convenient about it. Merely because his marriage had been arranged for financial considerations, everyone assumed he did not care about his wife. Did such an arrangement automatically preclude affection on both sides? Should not a love match be then called an inconvenient marriage? Perhaps he should make an announcement to that effect, perhaps he should—

"Leopold, are you attending me?"

"Of course, Mother. I apologize if I appear distracted. It has been an exhausting day."

"I can see that. I noticed you were limping as you came in. Now, as I was saying, much as I deplore his manners, one can enter into Mr. Prescott's feelings, at least on this occasion. You may not recall, but when Jane gave birth to Elizabeth, I was near out of my mind with worry. Of course your father did not give her a second thought . . ."

Odd, Leo thought, his leg *was* paining him. It was the first time in several months that the ache in the old wound had erupted. He certainly had not limped when Diana had called with Fenwick. Diana. Now that he thought of her, it was so clear to him that he had never loved her. He had been infatuated with Diana, blinded by her beauty, but he had never loved her, nor she him.

Love was that tender emotion reserved for one who shared your dreams and hopes for the future, someone who shared the small disappointments and everyday joys . . . love meant putting someone else's happiness and well-being above your own. And it dashed well didn't mean you couldn't love someone merely because you had come together through an arranged marriage.

"Leo, there is no need to glare at me so fiercely," Lavinia said, taken rather aback by the scowl on her son's face. "I was only trying to be helpful."

"And you have been. 'Tis only my leg is paining me," Leo said, and surprised her by suddenly leaning over and kissing her brow. "I promise I shall heed your advice. Now, will you give me leave? I am frightfully tired, but I promise we shall have ample time to talk tomorrow."

"Of course, my dear," Lavinia replied, and allowed him to help her up. She gazed up at his handsome face, and declared, "Perhaps you are not so like your father, after all. He had the most annoying habit of pretending to listen to me while thinking about something entirely different."

"Did he?" Leo asked as he escorted her from the room and up the broad staircase. He nodded to the footmen while trying to arrange in his mind what he would say to Gillian. He still thought Harry wrong. She could not possibly be thinking of leaving—why, she had not so much as mentioned Willowglen in months. And he distinctly remembered that when they were in London, she'd said she wanted to go *home*. Not to Willowglen but to Farthingale. This was the house she regarded as home. He knew in his heart that Harry must have gotten hold of an old bit of gossip . . . but it would not hurt to make certain Gillian understood just how much she had come to mean to him.

He paused outside his mother's room, hardly realizing how he came to be there, and bid her a good night. Then he hastened down the hall to the west wing and into his own bedchamber. Thurston had left a candelabra burning. By its gentle light, he could see his bed was turned down, his nightclothes laid out, and beyond the huge bed, the connecting door to his wife's chamber, standing ajar.

Leo strode across the room and called softly, "Gillian?"

He halted, his hand on the door. The tapers had all been extinguished, but there was sufficient moonlight streaming in the window to see that his wife was asleep, her tousled hair spread in red-gold waves across the pillow. Poor darling. She tired so easily these past two months. Usually she was in bed by nine or half past, and it had been nearly eleven when he'd seen Harry out. Given the strain of entertaining both their parents, the unpleasant scene at dinner, she must be utterly worn-out. As much as he wanted to talk to her, he had not the heart to waken her.

Taking care to be quiet, Leo crossed to the bed and tenderly drew the covers up about her shoulders. Brushing a stray curl from her brow, he whispered softly, "Sleep well, my darling."

His own sleep was long in coming. When he did doze off, he slept but fitfully, tossing and turning until near four in the morning before finally falling into a deep slumber. Thurston, entering his master's room the following day, saw the tangled bedcovers and discreetly withdrew. He knew his lordship's leg had been aching the night before, and it was obvious he'd not slept well. The valet conferred with Lady Wrexham, and between them they decided it would be best to allow the earl to sleep later than was his custom.

By the time Leo awoke, dressed, and sauntered below stairs, he found only his sister in the breakfast parlor. "Where is everyone?" he asked as he sat down at the table.

"Gillian took Mama and Papa Prescott to visit the tenants," Clarissa informed him while feeding bits of bacon to her pup. "She said to tell you they would be back this afternoon. Leo, I have been thinking. I meant to call my spaniel Oliver after Papa Prescott, which I thought would please him, but now that you have told him about the baby, well . . ."

"You mean I stole your thunder?" he asked as he accepted a cup of coffee from the footman.

She nodded. "Mama said naming a dog after someone was hardly a compliment, and perhaps she is right, but what am I to call this pup? Have you any suggestions?"

The spaniel, his coat the color of new leather, stood on his hind legs, his front paws on Clarissa's lap, looking up at her with doleful eyes.

"Beggar would seem to be appropriate," Leo replied, unfolding the daily paper. It was full of military news, but for once he was unable to concentrate on it, and after a few moments laid the paper aside. He wished he'd had a chance to speak to Gillian before she went out, but there would be time enough this afternoon. He was being fanciful, imagining there was any urgency. After all, he had waited five months, what was a few more hours?

"Leo? Is something troubling you?" Clarissa asked. "You have the strangest look on your face."

"Nothing in the world, save I was missing my wife. I've become accustomed to having breakfast with her, which is something you will understand once you are wed. Speaking of which, just how often did Harry call on you while you were in Bath?"

Clarissa blushed, her long lashes sweeping down to hide her gray eyes. "Did Mama tell you he was there visiting relatives?"

"No, minx, but I knew he was in Bath, and I saw the way you looked when he called last night. Clarissa, I don't mean to spoil your fun, but you are very young to be forming an attachment—"

"You won't forbid Harry to call, will you?" she pleaded, her eyes fastened on him with as mournful a look as her pup's. "I know Mama will not like it, but you are head of the family now, and if you approve—Leo, please don't say I must not see him."

"Goose! You must know Harry is like a brother to me. As for a match between you, it would be unexceptional, and if you are still of the same persuasion when you are a little older, I will gladly give you my blessing. But not until you have had a Season. You may think you know your mind now, and your heart, but believe me, you can be mistaken."

She rose and impulsively came around the table to hug him warmly. "Thank you, best of brothers. I know you are thinking of yourself and Miss Beauclerk, but this is different. Harry is like . . . well, I cannot explain it except to say that we are suited to each other in the same manner that you and Gillian are." She kissed his cheek, then danced toward the door. "I have to hurry, he is calling for me in half an hour."

"Clarissa?" he called, and when she paused, he asked with elaborate casualness, "Do you think Gillian and I are well suited? It seems an odd thing for you to say when you know ours was an arranged marriage."

She grinned at him. "I didn't think so at first, but last night—well, anyone could see how it was between you. The way you kept looking at each other, and every time you walked by her, you touched her shoulder or she reached for your hand. I thought it was very sweet."

Leo waited impatiently for his wife to return. He tried to concentrate on his breeding experiments, poring over the reports of several successful hybrids, but thoughts of Gillian kept intruding. He felt uneasy about her without knowing why. At half past two, he heard the sound of a carriage in the drive and breathed a sigh of relief. At last. He closed his books but remained behind his desk in the hope that Gillian would seek him out in the library, where they might have a few moments to converse in private.

He looked up expectantly as someone scratched on the door, but it was Partridge who stepped in. The butler looked unusually grave and said somberly, "My lord, there has been a most unfortunate accident. They are bringing Lady Wrexham home, sir, but the dowager sent a lad ahead to warn you."

Leo rose to his feet, ignoring the sudden throbbing in his leg. His face had turned ashen, and the tightness of his chest made breathing difficult, but he managed to ask levelly, "My wife?"

"She fainted, my lord, and struck her head when she fell. She was still unconscious when the lad left her," the butler replied distractedly. He cleared his throat and added, "The dowager suggested we send for Dr. Westcot, and I have taken the liberty of doing so."

"Thank you, Partridge," Leo said with a dismissive nod. "I shall be out directly." He started to sink back into his chair, when a thought occurred to him. "The boy my mother sent ahead—is he still here?"

"Yes, my lord. It is young Aubrey. He cut across the hills and was fair out of breath when he arrived. He's in the kitchen."

"Tell him I wish a word with him," Leo ordered. "I should like to hear firsthand what occurred."

"Yes, my lord."

Leo closed his eyes for a moment, uttering a silent, heartfelt prayer for Gillian's safety. Then Aubrey was shown into the library. He was perhaps ten and six, a tall, gangly boy who had not yet filled out his inches. A shock of red hair hung over his eyes, and his usual gap-toothed smile was missing. He stood near the door twisting a battered cap in his hands.

"Come in," Leo said, making an effort to set the boy at ease. "I just wish to ask you a question or two. You were present when Lady Wrexham fainted?"

The boy nodded.

"Can you tell me what happened? Where did the accident occur?"

"At Mrs. Craddock's," the lad replied. "I . . . I was helping 'er when 'er ladyship called."

Leo nodded encouragingly. The Craddocks had been pensioned off when the town house was sold, and he had given them a vacant crofter's cottage. He knew that Aubrey, who belonged to the neighboring farm, frequently helped the older couple with chores, and Gillian had encouraged him to do so by occasionally rewarding the boy a shilling.

"Well, my lord, Mrs. Craddock, she's been somewhat better, and she told her ladyship that if she'd drink a cuppa tea, she'd read the leaves for her. You know, tell her if'n it was a girl or a boy she was carrying," he explained in a rush, his face turning red. "There's some that say she has the gift. Well, my lady, she finished her tea and stood up, near ready to leave. She was talking to her pa and the dowager when Mrs. Craddock got done."

Trying hard to conceal his impatience, Leo said, "I understand. Please go on. What happened then?"

"Mrs. Craddock laughed and said the babe would be a fine, healthy boy—and then her ladyship, she jest . . . crumpled, swooned dead away. Her pa tried to catch her, but it happened so quick-like, and Lady Wrexham hit her head on the table when she fell. They tried to bring her about with smelling salts and stuff, but she jest . . . jest kept her eyes closed."

"I see. You did well, Aubrey. You may return to the kitchen now, and tell Cook I said you are to have whatever you wish."

"Yes, my lord, thank you, my lord," the boy muttered, backing as quickly from the library as he could.

Leo rose and paced the room. With every step he took, his leg throbbed, but he paid it no heed. He could think only of his wife. He knew the Craddocks' cottage lay five miles north of the house, and was half tempted to ride out to meet the carriage. He could probably intercept them on the road, but if he did so, he would only delay their progress—still, it was damnably hard waiting. He tried to reassure himself that Gillian might have already recovered from her faint.

The library door flew open, and a flustered Partridge shouted, "They're coming up the avenue, my lord, and Dr. Westcot right behind them!"

Leo's long-legged stride carried him across the room and out the door before the butler had time to recover his breath. In less than a minute, he was standing at the bottom of the stone steps, waiting impatiently as the carriage rolled up the avenue.

It was Leo who lifted his wife down from the carriage and carried her into the house. Even with the weight she'd recently gained, she seemed to him impossibly light and frail. He took her to the drawing room and laid her tenderly on the sofa. Unaware of his father-in-law or mother or the doctor crowding into the room behind him, he knelt beside the sofa and clasped her hand in his. "Gillian, my love . . ."

Dr. Westcot laid a hand on Wrexham's shoulder. "My lord, the best thing you can do is clear the room and allow me to examine her."

Leo could not be persuaded to leave Gillian's side, even to eat. His mother brought him a dish of biscuits and thin slices of ham, but the plate remained untouched. The doctor had said it might be an hour or several hours before Lady Wrexham regained consciousness, but he saw no cause for alarm. She would, he said, have a painful lump on her head, but, in his opinion, no lasting damage. Nevertheless, he promised to remain at Farthingale until she awoke.

For two hours, Leo sat in a chair drawn near the sofa, his hand clasping Gillian's, his eyes fixed steadily on her face. His mother, Gillian's father, the doctor, Sir Harry, and Clarissa had been in and out of the room, but he was seldom aware of their presence. If Oliver Prescott had any doubts about Leo's devotion to his daughter, they evaporated during that vigil.

Distraught, blaming himself for not being quick enough to catch his daughter when she fell, Oliver was also near to fainting. Lady Wrexham took him to the

breakfast parlor, insisted he eat, and poured the man a
stiff brandy. She sat with him, listening patiently as he
talked about Gillian and the doubts he'd suffered
watching her grow up without a mother. She refilled his
glass twice, and his mood turned melancholy.

"She's a good girl, my lady. Mayhap not the sort you'd
fancied for your son, but there's not a mean bone in her
body. Course she don't always listen to me—got a mind
of her own, my girl does. I'm right sorry I pulled caps
with her over staying here. It's plain his lordship
wouldn't allow her to do ought that would harm her. . . ."

Much touched, Lavinia later confided to her son that
perhaps there was something to be said for the merchant,
after all. Prescott might be ostentatious, and his manners
hardly those of a gentleman, but he was a good father—
which was a great deal more than she'd ever been able to
say about her own husband.

While the dowager was plying Oliver with brandy, and
occasionally taking a sip herself—for purely medicinal
reasons, of course—Leo prayed for his wife to recover.
He was so intent, so lost in his thoughts, that it was a
moment before he realized Gillian had suddenly spoken,
and even then he was not certain he had not imagined it.

She turned her head restlessly, murmured his name
again, and then her lashes fluttered open.

"Lie still, my dear. You've a nasty bump on your
head," he told her lightly, trying to keep the worry from
his voice.

"I . . . I fainted," she said, then her lashes closed again,
but only for a moment. She felt the reassuring clasp of
his hand, and her own fingers tightened within his. "Did
Papa bring me home?"

"He did and will be elated to know you're awake. Dr.
Westcot is waiting to see you, too. I should let him
know—"

"Not yet," she said, her hand tightening on his. "Stay with me for a moment. I was thinking of you."

"Were you? Probably because I have been sitting here beside you since they brought you home, and let me tell you, my girl, it was the longest three hours of my life. We must find out what caused you to faint, else I shall be afraid to let you out of my sight."

She smiled, but her eyes studied his face. Perhaps she was illusional from her fall, but the concern in his voice, the way he looked . . . almost like a gentleman in love. The notion was nonsensical, of course, mere wishful thinking on her part. She turned her head slightly so she could not see his gray eyes or the sharp planes of his face that she'd come to adore.

"There is no harm to the baby, if that is preying on your mind. Dr. Westcot examined you and said the child seems fine."

Gillian lifted her free hand and moved it protectively over her stomach. She should have known it was the baby he worried over. She abruptly recalled the old woman's prediction and told him, "Mrs. Craddock said it will be a boy, Leo. You shall have your heir after all."

"I told you—'tis an old Wrexham tradition. You doubted me?" he teased, hoping to dispel the underlying sadness he'd heard in her voice.

"I had . . . I wanted a girl," she replied softly. A girl would have meant at least another year at Farthingale, a year in which to make her husband so comfortable he would not wish her to leave. Her heart urged her to tell him the truth, to tell him she no longer wanted to return to Willowglen, that she could not bear to have an ocean between them. She bit her lip, resisting the temptation. Leo was too much the gentleman to protest if she wished to cry off from her bargain. He was so kind, so very kind. A tear crept from beneath her lashes.

Leo's heart constricted. Gillian sounded so forlorn, he

209

could resist the urge no longer. Leaving his chair, he gathered her in his arms so that her head rested securely against his shoulder, then dropped a featherlight kiss against her brow. "I am sorry if you are disappointed, my darling, but does it really matter so much? We can have a boy first, and then a girl, or half a dozen of each if that is what you desire. Gillian, I—are you crying?"

He turned her slightly so he could see her face, then kissed the tears from her lashes. "Lord, Gillian, don't do this to me. My love, I cannot endure to see you in tears."

She sniffed. Her mouth, wavering between a sob and a watery smile, caught his fingers and kissed them reverently. Her voice breaking, she said, "You . . . you called me your love."

He moved his hand beneath her chin and tenderly lifted her face, saying gently, "I shall apologize if you wish, but I am afraid I cannot change the way I feel about you."

Her large blue eyes threatened to overflow again. She sniffed, swallowed, and asked in a tremulous voice, "You are not merely saying so to make me feel better?"

In answer, he bent his head and kissed her thoroughly. All the love that he had stored so tidily behind his stoic British reserve poured forth, mingling with the anxiety that he'd endured for three hours and his overwhelming relief that she was not hurt. He was dimly conscious that her small hands had crept around his neck and that his kiss was returned with as much passion as any man could desire.

Clarissa opened the door, stared speechlessly for a moment, then softly shut the door again, leaning against it. She had been sent to discover if there was any change in Gillian's condition. A devilish grin curved the corners of her mouth. There certainly was, but she thought her brother might appreciate it if she didn't announce her sister-in-law's recovery just yet.

Clarissa saw Harry wander into the hall, searching for her. She put a finger to her lips and beckoned to him.

"What is it?" he asked in a hushed voice. "Has Gillian taken a turn for the worse?"

She shook her head and whispered, "Not at all. But I think Leo took your advice seriously—a bit too seriously." She eased the door open a crack, made certain the couple inside were still entwined in the same position, then stepped aside so Harry could see.

He peered in the door, then hastily eased it shut. With an arm about Clarissa's shoulders, he hurried her down the hall. "You little imp. Have you no better manners than to spy on your brother?"

She laughed, completely unrepentant. "I only came to see about Gillian. How was I to know my very proper brother meant to seduce her in the drawing room? Only wait until the next time he lectures me on propriety. I shall have a thing or two to say to him." She looked back down the hall. "How long do you think we should give them before telling Mama and Papa Prescott?"

"I don't see that another five minutes would hurt. Then we shall go knock on the door and look *very* surprised that Gillian has recovered."

"Do you mean I am not to tease him?" she asked, glancing provocatively up at him from beneath her lashes.

"Precisely," he said, and tweaked a curl as though she were one of his sisters rather than a very lovely young lady. A pity, he thought, that she was not a little older, or he would take his own advice and tell her exactly how he felt about her. Restraining the impulse, he challenged her instead to a game of chess after dinner.

"Done, but if you lose, you will have to stay and help me take Beggar for a walk."

In the library, unaware that their privacy was about to end, Gillian nestled in her husband's arms. Her fingers

211

toyed with the buttons on his coat. "I wish you would have told me," she complained. "I have been praying that I might have a girl because then I wouldn't have to go back to Willowglen as I had promised you I would."

He kissed her brow. "But I told you—even before we wed—that I hoped you would change your mind."

"I know, but that was the sort of thing you would say, even if you didn't mean it. And I knew about Miss Beauclerk, so . . ."

"Are you going to hold that against me?" he asked. "I realize I was six kinds of a fool. My only excuse is that I had not met anyone quite like you before." His arm tightened about her as though he never intended to let her go. "Egad, but 'tis frightening to think how close I came to losing you."

She rested her head against his shoulder and looked up at him. Love glowed in her eyes and echoed in her voice as she said, "I don't think you need ever worry about that."

"And Willowglen? Are you certain you no longer wish to return there?"

She shook her head. "It seems so very long ago . . . maybe one day, when our son is older, we could travel to America for a visit. I think you would like it—oh! I think our son approves."

At the same moment a tap sounded on the door, then Clarissa stepped in with Sir Harry behind her.

"Gillian!" she squealed. "Oh, thank heavens, you are revived. We have been so worried." And with her eyes full of mischief, she asked, "Leo, how long has she been awake?"

Suppressing a grin, he looked down at his wife, who was blushing adorably. "Not nearly long enough."

"Here you are," Lavinia said with an odd little laugh as she came into the room on the arm of Mr. Prescott.

"Clarissa, you naughty, naughty girl—why did you not . . . not . . . Oliver, what was I saying?"

Appealed to, her escort considered the matter, then shook his head. "Darn if I know, Lavinia, but I think . . . think we should sit down."

"Good heavens," Leo muttered. "I believe Mama is tipsy."

"In her cups," Clarissa declared with a giggle, but she hurried to her mother's side and assisted the dowager to a chair. Lavinia sprawled in a most undignified, unladylike position.

"Our dear Gillian is re-recovered," Lavinia pronounced, her words slightly slurred. "Calls for a celebration. Leopold! Ring for Minna. Champagne for everyone."

"Champagne," Oliver echoed as Sir Harry helped him to a chair beside the dowager. "Drink to Gillian—that's the ticket."

"I think perhaps some black coffee would be more beneficial," Leo suggested.

"Nonsense," Harry told him. "It appears to me you have a lot to celebrate, old man. Besides, the damage has been done. One more drink won't hurt."

"Oh, please, Leo," Clarissa begged. "One toast to Gillian. I've never had champagne before, and Mama won't object—not now."

Leo gave up the battle. "One toast, and then I am taking Gillian and tucking her in bed. She needs her rest."

"And you, too, no doubt," Harry replied blandly.

Minna brought a bottle into the drawing room, looked slightly askance at the occupants, then slipped back to the kitchen to report the strange way the family was behaving.

Sir Harry did the honors, filling each of the glasses,

and then lifting his in a salute. "To you both, long health and happiness."

Beneath his breath, so quietly only Gillian could hear him, Leo added, "To you, my love, and our inconvenient marriage."